Desperate Journey

JIM MURPHY

SCHOLASTIC PRESS *NEW YORK*

LIBRARY OF CONGRESS CATALOGING-IN-PUBLICATION DATA

Murphy, Jim, 1947–

Desperate journey / by Jim Murphy. — 1st ed/ p. cm.

Summary: In the mid-1800s, with both her father and her uncle in jail on an alleged assault charge, Maggie, her brother, and her ailing mother rush their barge along the Erie Canal to deliver their heavy cargo or lose everything.

ISBN 0-439-07806-7

[1. Riverboats — Fiction.   2. Family life — Fiction.   3. Erie Canal (N.Y.) — Fiction.]

I. Title.PZ7.M9535Des 2006 [Fic] — dc 2006002526

10   9   8   7   6   5   4   3   2   1   06   07   08   09   10

Special thanks to Andy Kitzmann, Assistant Director and Curator of the Erie Canal Museum in Syracuse, New York, for his expert consultation on this novel. The image on page 272 was originally published in *Marco Paul's Travels on the Erie Canal* by Jacob Abbott, and is reproduced courtesy of Heart of the Lakes Publishing. The map on pages iv-v, *Map of the State of New York showing its Water and Rail Road Lines*, was published in 1854 in the Report of the State Engineer and Surveyor. This map was reproduced by permission of the Erie Canal Museum, New York, www.eriecanalmuseum.org. It may not be reproduced or republished without the museum's express written permission. The map on page 270 is by Jim McMahon, copyright © 2006 by Scholastic.

The display type was set in P22 Stanyan Bold.

The text type was set in 13-pt Filosofia Regular.

Book design by Marijka Kostiw

Printed in the U.S.A. First edition, October 2006

FOR A TEACHING GUIDE GO TO WWW.SCHOLASTIC.COM

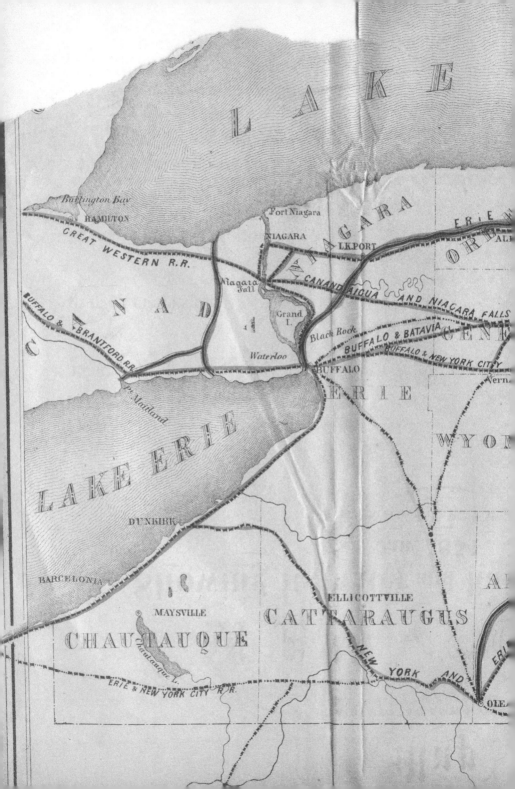

Contents

The Erie Canal
1848

At THE BEGINNING OF THE NINETEENTH CENTURY,

people in the United States were already streaming

west in search of new land and new opportunities.

To speed settlers to their destinations,

many states east of the Mississippi River began

digging canals. New York State built what was

then the longest artificial waterway in history,

an engineering feat that stretched over three hundred and sixty miles from Albany to Buffalo.

By 1848, when this story takes place, the Big Ditch was home and workplace to more than 20,000 people, a tough, hardworking, and colorful collection of individuals who overcame incredible obstacles and helped shape a young nation's destiny and spirit.

Like a Mule 1

Maggie plodded along behind the mules, one muddy boot step after the other. I'm no different than these dumb, stupid animals, she thought, as she stepped into their hoofprints to avoid the deepest mud.

She used the sleeve of her canvas jacket to wipe rainwater from her face, then flicked the whip angrily to sting the trailing mule's rump. Issachar shivered at the whip's bite, and immediately lengthened his stride, snapping the line to the boat taut. With no time to adjust her pace, Maggie's next step sank into a good six inches of slippery, fresh mud.

"What's going on there?" her papa barked from the darkness behind her. His voice was a mixture of annoyance and concern at the sudden jolt to his boat. Papa's temper had teetered on the edge since his fight with the Canadian in November.

"Slow, boys, slow," Maggie whispered.

Issachar's head turned so that one gleaming black eye fixed on her, as if to tell her to make up her silly mind.

"Sorry, Issachar," Maggie murmured as the mule readjusted his pace.

"Better," Papa grumbled, followed by a now familiar mournful sigh.

"I'd never do *that*," Eamon announced loudly. Her brother had hurried on deck the moment he'd felt the boat shudder.

"It was a mistake," Maggie called back. "Hardly even a wiggle —"

"Wasn't talkin' to *you*. But I'd still drive steady and not shake the boat at every turn."

"Okay, you two," Papa said impatiently. "Not now."

It had been an ongoing contest between them since Eamon turned nine. He wanted to drive the mules more and had pounced on any sign of weakness from Maggie. And while she hated the sameness of the job, she would rather fall down dead on the towpath than let him win.

Just then a gust of wind whipped the rain around, and a freezing cold snake of liquid slithered down Maggie's back. "Golly jeez lickspigot!" she yelped loudly.

"See, told ya," Eamon blurted out. "A girl can't drive mules proper without makin' a silly fuss. But I could. I'd drive'm all day and all night and not say peep or nothin'."

"Some cold water went down my back!"

"So what?" he demanded. He paused to think of something more hurtful to say. "A real driver wouldn't be scared by a little water!"

"I wasn't scared —"

"That's what you said when you stepped on that snake. And it was dead!"

"Maggie," their momma said, coming on deck from the cabin. "What's going on out here?" Her voice sounded exhausted.

"She can't even fight for herself," Eamon exclaimed. "A *real* driver would, but she needs her momma —"

"Do not —"

"Can't a man read in peace?" Uncle Hen asked, poking his head from the stable door.

"Eamon's being a pain. Like usual."

"And she's makin' a big fuss. Like usual."

"I am not!"

"Am, too!"

"Enough!" their papa bellowed and a perfect silence followed. "You, Eamon, will get to drive when I tell you. And bothering your sister won't make it happen any sooner, hear?"

Eamon grunted his answer.

"Hear?"

"Yes, Papa. But Maggie's always —"

"Eamon!" Papa said firmly. "Go below with your mother and not another word." Maggie chuckled in triumph. "And you, Maggie. Pay attention to what you're doing before you run the mules into the Canal."

"Yes, Papa," she said glumly.

After this, Maggie stretched her long legs out to get back in step with the mules as a dark cloud settled over her. She might expect a sharp word or two from Momma, who seemed always on the lookout for some mistake of Maggie's. But it was only since November and the fight that Papa had begun to change toward her, seemed at times disappointed and distant. Those were the moments when Maggie felt most alone.

It was worse at night, like now. Darkness turned the Canal into a flat, gray ribbon that disappeared into dead black ahead and behind. If only there was something to take her mind off her family.

She glanced up briefly and there — as if to mock her — was a break in the trees, enough to reveal a wood fence and, off in the inky distance, a faint glow of yellow light. What house was that? she wondered. What were the folks inside doing? The woods took up again to blot out this small sign of life on land, but it had set

Maggie thinking . . . of a small, neat house on dry solid land . . . of a real bed that didn't rock back and forth all night. . . .

The lead mule, James, snorted loudly and Maggie's thoughts came back to the Canal. They had gone through Rome at seven that morning, with Uncle Henry driving the mules and Papa at the sweep, steering the boat. "We need to make up time, Hen," Papa had announced. They had lost half a day waiting to pass through the Utica locks, plus two whole days from Momma being sick. "Five days to Buffalo or bust."

"We're doing fine, Tim," Hen had replied. "We'll make that bonus easy."

"Can't take any chances . . ." Papa's voice had trailed off, but Maggie knew what he was thinking. He'd lost almost all their savings in that fight with Long-fingered John, and had borrowed money against their boat to make it through winter. That loan was coming due at the end of the month, and if they missed the payment they'd lose the *Betty*.

That awful possibility was never talked about but was always around to worry them. It was there in her papa's drinking and his faraway looks, in the way Momma criticized her for every little thing, in the way that everyone always seemed nervous and snappy. "This April weather's changeable," Papa added. "A big storm could delay us and then what? We need to push'm today to be safe."

Papa kept Issachar and James pulling at a steady three miles per hour all day. Even the second team, Rudy and Tom, managed to keep to a lively pace despite being younger and smaller. Papa had hoped to cover thirty miles before stopping, but Maggie guessed they'd only made twenty-five or so.

Twenty-five miles from Rome would put them near . . . where? The route of the Canal — the sequence of locks and farms, taverns and stores — that she should know without having to think on it seemed to have evaporated. As if willed away. Then it came to her: If her addition was correct, they should be near Dalrumple's Tavern.

The thought of Dalrumple's lifted Maggie from her gloom. Tom Dalrumple had built his tavern on the towpath in 1819 to entice the Canal diggers, especially the boisterous Irish bogtrotters. He'd died of the cholera in 1826, but his wife, Jozina — known to all as Jozie — had run the place ever since. Seven days a week for twenty-two years.

Jozie was a big woman, taller than most men, with short black hair, piercing brown eyes, and a voice both deep and commanding. Not many brawls took place inside her tavern, and even Eamon listened sharp when Jozie told him to stop running off at the mouth.

Most important to Maggie, Jozie was also the news crier of the Canal, up on all that was happening along its three hundred and sixty-odd miles. And, oh, could Jozie spin out a lively story. Even something routine like a boatman getting drunk and falling into the Canal sounded dramatic and important when Jozie told it.

There was a rustle of branches to the right of the towpath, but Maggie could make out only the great, dense barrier of trees. A twig snapped, and something scurried along. Probably just a muskrat.

That was when Maggie remembered the big willow that had fallen partway over during a storm last summer. It was two miles shy of Dalrumple's, and Maggie was certain they hadn't passed it yet. That meant they were farther from the tavern than she'd figured.

Her spirits drooped again, and she shivered inside her jacket. Issachar's breathing was louder now, the long day's pulling finally catching up to the four-year-old mule. Her papa, distracted as he'd been since the fight, would soon hear Issachar and have her stop the team for the night. He wouldn't want to risk injuring him, not with the boat at stake.

From behind she heard her momma's tired voice, then her father's reply, "Up 'round Harley's Bend. We'll tie up there." So he had heard Issachar. Her brother's higher-pitched voice cut in between the two adults talking, then there was laughter from all three. She felt herself being pushed away. As if the towline was a mile long and she nothing but a distant, unrelated observer of their lives. Even the meow of their gray-and-black tomcat, Marcus, seemed far away.

"Maggie," her father called. "Next post we'll tie up."

"Yes, Papa," she answered. Before the fight, it would have been "Maggie darlin'," a small thing, but enough to drive away all the loneliness.

"Just a little more, boys," she told the mules.

A vision of the opening they'd just passed and a red rectangle of paper pushed into Maggie's thoughts. A red poster from last summer with crude writing nailed to the wood fence there. Why couldn't she recall the message?

The first rock went whirring over her head to plunk harmlessly into the Canal. A second caught Issachar in the side and brought a frightened snort from him. Then he was braying frantically and quickstepping, trying to turn as a third rock got him in the shin.

"Whoa, Issa —" A rock hit Maggie so hard in the cheek that she toppled over and landed in the muddy towpath.

She tried to call for help, but no sound came out. Instead, the metallic taste of blood filled her mouth and she heard the mocking call of a boy, "Get away, ya dirty canal girl!" followed by a chorus of taunts from two or three other kids.

Maggie realized that both Issachar and James were backing up toward her as more rocks sailed in. She rolled away through the slime to avoid the mules' huge, stamping hooves, heard the heavy leather squeak of their traces getting closer.

"Anna, take the sweep!" Papa roared as he leaped from the boat and pounded across the towpath. "Hit my boat, ya little —"

Next came her uncle's insistent voice, "Stop, boys, stop, ya hear? Stop now. Whoa there. . . ." He'd come out of the stable, taken in the situation, and, dropping his book to the deck, jumped from the boat to grab at James's harness. "Get out of the way, Maggie!" he yelled as the terrified animals pulled him along through the mud.

Her momma was on deck now, straightening the steering sweep before the boat drifted across the Canal. Then Momma was yelling, too, though all Maggie could hear was her father's string of cusses and the sound of small feet retreating rapidly through the woods.

"The lines!" her Momma was shouting urgently. "Before the mules get dragged!"

Maggie tried to push herself up, slipped, and nearly went facedown in the mud. She tried again and managed to struggle to her feet. Almost immediately, she felt as if she might throw up as she tasted more blood. She leaned over and began sucking in gulps of cool air.

Her uncle managed to stop the mules' backpedaling a few feet short of Maggie, but the beasts were still agitated, still prancing wildly, as they struggled to break free. The *Betty*, meanwhile, moved steadily up-canal, its loaded weight of seventy tons like some giant, unstoppable boulder. Maggie started searching for her whip, but gave that up when a sharp hoof kicked out at her.

"The lines!" Momma called as the boat slid even with Maggie. "Cut the lines!"

Maggie leaped aside to avoid another hoof, then scurried ahead to grab Issachar's halter. As soon as she did, the mule pumped his head several times in panic, lifting Maggie off the ground a foot or two with each jerk.

Uncle Henry had James quieted and was tugging at him to move forward again. "Come on, James," he said in a soothing voice. "Come on. Everything is fine now, everything is fine."

Maggie noticed the boat was now ahead of them.

In just a few moments, the two hundred feet of towline would snap taut and drag the animals and whoever was holding on to them into the black water. The lines needed to be cut.

Only then did she realize that Uncle Hen was wearing his long underwear, which meant he didn't have a knife with him. She fumbled in the pocket of her dress for her knife, but couldn't find it. Probably left it on the shelf near her bunk.

Her head screamed for her to tell about the knife, but her mouth refused to confess. Papa would never forgive her. Eamon would never let her forget. There was only one thing she could think to do. She smacked Issachar a good hard slap on his hindquarters, and the startled mule vaulted forward, nudging James into motion. Uncle Henry hurried to stay with them. "Thata boy, thata boy," he said.

Maggie only had time to see the mules and Uncle Hen moving ahead before her feet went out from under her and once more she was in the mud. It took a while for her to calm her thoughts enough to look up. She was relieved to see that the mules had established a regular pace and were staying with the boat.

Her father emerged from the woods and instantly lit out after the *Betty*, his boots hitting the mud with a thick, sucking sound. "Maggie, what did you . . ." He and the entire scene were just shapes to Maggie, moving away from her.

A chorus of indistinct voices came floating next. "Any damage to the boat?" Papa wanted to know, answered by Momma's "A window or two broken, that's all." The adults exchanged other breathless comments. Then another voice found her. "See, I told ya she wasn't no good at driving. . . ."

The red poster. Now she remembered the hastily scrawled words: *Canawlers Go PEE sumplace ellse.* How could she have ever forgotten that sign and the mean, rat-faced kids who went along with it, taunting her from the other side of the fence?

She retrieved her whip, then began hunting for her hat, only to discover it still sitting primly atop her head. She let loose a mighty string of pent-up cusses that no one in the universe heard, then hurried to catch up with the boat.

She could imagine how she would be greeted: Didn't you hear them? I wouldn't've let those dung eaters get away, Pa. You best stop daydreaming and pay attention. And so on. And on. And on.

The side of her face throbbed, but a quick probe with a muddy finger told her she hadn't lost any teeth.

That was something at least, she thought, spitting out gritty blood. She slowed down as she drew nearer the *Betty*. Momma was still at the sweep with Eamon right beside her, a cozy silhouette that made Maggie jealous. Papa and Uncle Henry each had a mule by the harness and were guiding them along at a slow walk.

Suddenly, her face grew hot as another thought came to her. Tomorrow, the story of her encounter with a handful of little kids would be shared with Jozie, and then Jozie would share it with every boat crew that visited her tavern. And they'd share it with every lock tender and storekeeper along the way.

She wanted to disappear, to melt into the night and wake up in another town away from her family, away from the Canal. Any place would do. But where exactly was that? She felt her cheek where the rock had hit her.

"You okay?" her mother asked when she noticed Maggie, though she sounded too exhausted to really care.

"I'm fine," Maggie answered in a very small voice.

She glanced at Papa, hoping he'd say something — anything — to make her feel like she belonged. Like she was a part of the family again. Instead, he said, "Harley's should be coming up soon. Eamon, you'll help Uncle Hen tend to the mules while Maggie gets herself cleaned up."

Eamon gave a crisp "yes, sir" and rushed up to the stable to measure out oats.

Maggie let loose a sigh every bit as mournful as one of her father's. There was no place to run to, no place else for her but there. Trapped is what she was. Trapped with her family and the mules and the *Betty*. Trapped on the Erie Canal.

Thinking and 2
Dreaming

"**B**ridge!" Uncle Hen boomed from the towpath, answered immediately by Papa's own, "Bridge!" It was the warning to anyone on deck to look sharp because the boat was approaching one of the many low bridges spanning the Canal.

Below in the cabin, Maggie was scraping leavings from breakfast into the slops pail. Everybody else dumps garbage out the window and into the water, she grumped. But not us! Her momma had banned that long ago. Spitting and tossing bottles out the window were also forbidden.

The hazy light filtering through the cabin windows was suddenly extinguished as the boat slid quietly under the bridge. The darkness lasted a scant few seconds, just enough time to remind Maggie of last night's attack.

Why was it, she wondered, that her thoughts were always drifting away from the here and now without her permission? The blaze of a flower's color, for instance, could bring an image of Grandma Peg in her flower-patterned dress stretched out peacefully in her coffin.

There was one good reason to remember last night, Maggie told herself, as she spied her face in the tiny mirror. The aching purple welt on her cheek. She would get even with those sneaky, rat-faced little . . .

"Maggie, watch what you're about!" Momma snapped as Maggie dropped a great heap of half-eaten flapjacks, eggshells, and sodden coffee grounds onto the floor. Momma may have been feeling poorly these past weeks, but she could still flare up hotter than a blacksmith's fire when anyone made a mess.

Maggie fumed at her momma's sharp words, but shifted her anger to those kids. If they hadn't attacked us, she told herself, and set me thinking on revenge, I wouldn't have been distracted.

"You clean that up good now, and don't leave a speck."

"Yes, Momma," Maggie replied in a sullen tone. Why was it that Momma hardly ever reprimanded Eamon about the messes *he* made?

Maggie finished scooping up the debris, then dried and buffed the floor until it glowed. No use doing half a job, since Momma, if dissatisfied in the least, would make her do it all over again.

Her mother leaned forward from her place at the

fold-down table and cast a critical eye on the floor. Maggie was certain those piercing green eyes could see a half-speck of dirt at fifty paces. To Maggie's relief, Momma nodded in satisfaction. "Good," she said. "Jozie might come aboard when we stop, and I don't want her thinking we're common."

Maggie exhaled gratefully at this bit of welcome news. This was followed immediately by a pang of concern. Would Papa still feel comfortable at Dalrumple's, what with his fight being the big story of the past year?

Momma had already settled back to her sewing. The stitches, Maggie could see, were close-spaced and infinitely regular, like a professional tailor's. And she was only fixing an old pair of Eamon's work pants.

Her mother wanted everything to be perfect — the boat, the meals, the stitches she made in their clothes. She even worked hard to hide every trace of her Irish accent because she thought it coarse. You would think by the way she fussed that she was some dainty Washington, D.C., hostess and President Polk was coming to dinner.

Maggie smiled at the notion of associating the word "dainty" with her momma. Momma could steer the boat as well as Papa, handle the mules as easily as Uncle Hen, drive for hours in any weather, and still sit up late telling stories.

Of course, Momma hadn't been so energetic this trip. She'd been sick enough near Fultonville and again at Fort Plain that Papa was forced to tie up so she could rest, even though it put the bonus and the boat in jeopardy. But most times, Momma could keep up with the men in every way. In fact, she'd met Papa in a tavern — which was unusual, since women didn't generally frequent such low places.

Maggie had heard the story so many times that she knew the details by heart. It was the Green Dragon in Albany, a block from the Canal and filled with men, noise, and cigar smoke. Momma was Anna McDonagh at the time, and unmarried, and she'd gone there to meet a friend. When she brushed past a table where Tim Haggarty was celebrating a fast haul with Hen and some friends, he called out a greeting.

Exactly what Papa said had been forgotten over the years, most likely because of its rude content. Whatever it was, Anna turned and stared down at Tim as he sat, drink in hand and a smirk on his handsome face.

"Oh?" she asked in a whisper. "Were you talking to me, sir? I missed your comment."

Tim flashed a triumphant smile and began to repeat his request. He hadn't even gotten three words out when she punched him hard enough to knock him sprawling across the sawdusted floor. Was the only time anyone had ever knocked Tim Haggarty to the ground — that is, until Long-fingered John did it in November.

"Check Uncle Hen's bunk, Maggie," her mother said, pushing into her daughter's thoughts. "His drawers will be muddy from last night" — she clicked her tongue disapprovingly — "and knowing Hen, he probably slept in them, so his bedding'll need washing, too."

Maggie said yes and went to leave the cabin, but pulled up at the stairs. "Momma, when you punched Papa that time in Albany, did he really fall in love with you that instant the way you always say? Papa gets mad so quick, I'd think he'd at least cuss some."

"What made you think of that?" Momma wanted to know.

Maggie shrugged. "Just wondered, is all."

Momma gave a little grunt as she sat straight up to think. "Well, if you must know, he got up sputtering and cussing, and mad as a hornet."

"And?"

"And I told him he needed to mind his manners, which he did, and that's about all there is to the story. Satisfied? Now get to your chores."

Momma had a pleasing round face, with cheeks a permanent rose blush and dotted with freckles. When she smiled, her face had an inviting, attractive glow. But when she stared at a person — as she now stared at Maggie — it seemed like one of those No TRESPASSING signs hung along a farmer's property.

"You mean Papa cussed a little, then fell in love?" Maggie snapped her fingers. "I don't see how —"

"Maggie, we don't have time for this now. We've a bonus to make, remember?"

"But, Momma —"

"No buts. Toss those leavings and get to that wash. I put some things to soak in the tub." Her mother went back to her sewing, clearly finished reliving history out loud.

Shut out and pushed away was how Maggie once again felt as she went on deck. And just when she'd gotten Momma to the part she'd always wondered about, that mysterious moment when two people fall in love.

As she emptied and rinsed the slops pail, she heard Papa ask Hen if Tom was favoring his leg. A quick glance told Maggie the mule was fine. Papa's nervous, is all, she told herself. And not about Tom's leg, either. It's the bonus that's got him edgy. And the visit at Dalrumple's.

He's no need to be so nervous about going to Jozie's, she realized as she went forward. His fight is old news now. I'm the story of the day, Maggie reminded herself.

Eamon, Maggie noticed, was sitting atop Rudy, singing "The E-RI-E" in a high, strained voice: "Oh the E-ri-e was a-rising/ And the gin was getting low/ And I scarcely think we'll get a drink/ Till we get to Buf-fa-lo. . . ." She couldn't tell whether Rudy's twitching ears were the result of his born skittishness or Eamon's off-key singing.

The air in the stable was already heavy with the smell of mule sweat, oats, and leather, so Maggie hurried to gather up Uncle Hen's muddy things. Momma was right; he'd slept in his sopping clothes, so his thin bunk mattress and sheet needed washing, too.

The washtub, as promised, was at the bow, already loaded with the rest of the day's wash. She dumped Uncle Hen's things into the tub, then set to working each garment against the ribs of the washboard.

Kneeling over her work just a few moments, her arms pumping up and down, reminded Maggie all over again how tedious the chore was. Still, there was one part of washing that Maggie enjoyed. She could escape the boat and her family by imagining herself living on one of the many farms they passed. She could see herself watching the sunset from the narrow front porch or getting water from the pump that looked like some sort of long-legged metal bird. And the neighbors — maybe they wouldn't know she was a Canal girl and be as friendly to her as they might be with anybody.

"Bridge!" Eamon shouted gleefully, adding, "Beat you to it, Uncle Hen. I called first!"

"Bridge," her papa answered.

Of course, whenever she asked Momma about living in the world away from the Erie Canal, her mother's reply always came with a warning. "We're different, Maggie, and they'll never let us forget it." Maggie thought there had to be someplace, some village or town, where she would fit in. But where?

After Maggie had all of the items scrubbed and hung on the line that stretched from bow to stern, she set to sweeping the deck. Tom gave a loud snort just as he was ducking under the branches of the falling-over willow. Two miles to Dalrumple's.

A weary sadness settled over Maggie when she recalled what Hen had said after his last trip to New York City. That just standing on a busy street there watching hundreds of people bustling about, seeing all of the tall buildings, hearing the jumbled sounds of a big city made his mind race. "Some don't like the pace," he told Maggie. "Makes them nervous. But I do."

She wondered if there might just be a place for her there, but almost immediately shuddered when she realized how far away she'd be from the Canal. . . .

"Maggie, duck, girl!" Papa screamed.

Maggie spun around, caught a fleeting glimpse of the thick braces of a bridge rushing at her face, closed her eyes, and ducked. Her arm slammed down hard against the roof of the stable as the bridge swept over her head, missing her by inches.

"Maggie, you alright?" Papa asked.

"Yes," she answered, her breath coming in fast gulps.

"See, told ya! She can't even go under a bridge without makin' a silly fuss!"

"I was sweeping the deck. . . ."

"A real canaler wouldn't let that happen!"

"Eamon," Papa shouted, "mind what you're doing there! I should have sung out louder."

The look on his face said Eamon didn't believe that for a second, but he knew better than to correct Papa.

"Sorry, Papa," she mumbled. "I should've been listening better."

"You lost someplace, Maggie?" he asked.

"Just thinking, Papa."

Her father grunted softly, his dark eyes fixed on an approaching coal barge that had wandered out too far as it came around a turn. "Thinking and dreaming are fine, Maggie," he said. "But they can get you in trouble on the water."

Was he talking about the near accident just now, she wondered, or remembering last night? Her back stiffened and Maggie was about to defend herself, when he took hold of her right hand and put it on the sweep. "You steer for a bit while I check on your momma," he said.

He took the broom from her as Maggie stood there blinking at the suddenness of it all. Maybe he wasn't really disappointed with her about last night, she thought. Otherwise, why was he giving her control of the boat? As if he'd read her thoughts, Papa added, "Could use a drop about now, too," then disappeared below. "Look sharp, now."

"I will, Papa."

"Why does *she* get to steer?" Eamon wailed when he noticed her alone at the sweep.

Oh, shut up, she wanted to say, but didn't. This was no time to get distracted with a silly fight, not after nearly having her head shaved off. She kept her eyes riveted on the water before her.

Eamon's complaining went on several minutes and then Uncle Hen, clearly as tired of his whining as Maggie was, told Eamon to get off Rudy and walk.

They went under another bridge and around a big bend where the diggers had cut right through a great hill covered with pine trees. Maggie had made many such turns before without trouble, but today she felt nervous and unsure of herself. She breathed a sigh of relief as she negotiated the turn and the boat entered a long, straight section of water. A mile off, Maggie spotted a small gathering of boats and a familiar cluster of buildings.

"Dalrumple's!" she sang out.

Eamon's head snapped to attention as he searched ahead. "I would've seen it first if I'da been on Rudy —"

"We're almost to Dalrumple's," Maggie called down to the cabin.

Papa reemerged, drink in hand. "I'll take her in," he said. He took a quick sip before grabbing the sweep.

Eamon took the leads from his uncle, after which Uncle Hen bounded on deck and picked up a pole. Maggie took the other pole and stood on the outer deck, ready to slow the boat's drift. Already her heart was beating fast over the visit. In anticipation and dread.

They were a quarter mile from the tavern, drifting

lazily. She glanced back at Papa and saw his eyes narrowed, his jaw tight. She looked toward the tavern again, which was when she spotted the brown-and-yellow boat tied among the others. She didn't have to look twice to know who owned that boat. Long-fingered John.

Something Terribly Wrong

3

It felt as if it took hours to cover the final quarter mile to Dalrumple's. The deliberateness of their boat's pace, the very routine of tying up and getting the boarding plank out all worked to heighten Maggie's anxiety.

"Eamon," Papa said, "take Rudy and Tom to the barn and ask Samuel to check Tom's leg." He took a sip of cider, his eyes darting to the door of the tavern.

Maggie felt her heart racing, knowing the man who beat up Papa was inside and probably bragging to anybody who'd listen. She remembered the blur of fists striking out and a sickening wave of guilt swept over her.

Most of her father's fights were over in a flash. A punch or two and his opponent realized the mistake of challenging Tim Haggarty. But Papa and Long-fingered John were so evenly matched that they traded vicious punches with no letup for thirty long minutes. Iron-hard fists slamming into flesh.

She hated that Papa had fights, even though he only fought to defend weaker, more timid captains against Canal bullies. Yet she was always proud of him after each victory, and she felt somehow connected to his strength. As if nothing could harm her. But as last year's fight with Long-fingered John dragged on, Maggie had thought for the first time ever that Papa might lose. Would lose.

And that was exactly when Long-fingered John caught Papa with an uppercut to the chin, followed by a crushing right to his nose that put Papa stretched out on the ground.

There had been a gasp from the crowd, followed by stunned silence as Papa tried to raise himself, faltered, then flopped over onto his back. Long-fingered John stood over Papa, panting hard and spitting out, "Get up, ye . . . ye blasted stupid mick. Get . . . up!"

Some in the crowd began encouraging her father to continue, and Eamon was bawling out, "Pa, get up, get up! You can still whup him, Pa!"

Papa managed to roll over and push himself to his hands and knees. He was dazed, with a great, long string of bloody snot stretching from his face to the dirt between his hands. Immediately, Maggie felt that she was responsible for what had happened, that her lapse of faith had doomed him.

Eamon was still urging his father to fight on, but tears were streaming down his cheeks. Maggie was crying, too. For his pain and his damaged body, of course, but also for her shame.

"Now, Tim." It was her mother's warning voice that brought Maggie back to the present at Dalrumple's. Her mother had come on deck and seen the brown-and-yellow boat. "No fighting here. Not at Jozie's."

"I've no intention of fighting, Anna." He drained his glass and set it down carefully on the cabin roof. "Not unless I'm provoked."

"I mean it, Tim," Momma said, her voice weary, but with a bit of steel to it. "You might want to temper your drinking some, too. We've a load due in four days. . . ."

"I know," Papa replied impatiently. He went down the wobbly plank to the towpath where he waited. "On the eighteenth. I've no intention of missing the date or the bonus."

Eamon wandered off toward the barn, leading Rudy and Tom. He was, as far as Maggie could tell, completely unaware that Long-fingered John was nearby. Just then, the door to Dalrumple's banged open and Jozie emerged, her arms wide in greeting, a worried cast to her eyes.

"I've been waiting!" Jozie nearly shouted. "This has been the longest winter on record, let me tell you." She wrapped Momma in a great hug before commenting on her peaked appearance. Next she embraced Uncle Hen, Papa, and finally Maggie. As she pulled back from Maggie she noticed the fresh bruise. "Lord Almighty, girl, where'd you get that?"

Maggie bowed her head and put her hand to her cheek. Fortunately, Papa was quick to explain. "Took a rock last night. Got the mules, too, and the *Betty*. No real damage done though, right, Maggie?"

Trust that Papa would lump her injury in with what happened to his animals and precious boat. But at least he didn't say she'd been daydreaming.

"Smarts a little, that's all," Maggie said, shrugging. "Still have all my teeth."

"Was a pack of rotten kids," Papa said.

"Down by Harley's," Momma added. "Maggie and Hen had a heck of a time calming the mules."

"That was mostly Maggie," Uncle Hen explained. "I was in my drawers and sliding along in the mud. Was Maggie got the beasts going before we went into the Canal."

"By Harley's?" Jozie said. "Hmmm. That would be those Herkimer brats. We hear stories about them and their mischief all the time." Jozie looked again at Maggie. "And my, haven't you gone and grown up all of a sudden! A beauty, just like your momma."

Maggie felt herself blushing at the compliment and at suddenly being made the hero of the attack. It would have been nice if someone had said something like that last night when she felt so awful, but no never mind that now. What counted was that Jozie was told about the incident in a way that hadn't embarrassed Maggie.

Jozie's voice dropped low. "He's inside now, Tim. Him and his crew and another." The tone of her voice seemed to be asking Papa to hold his anger in check.

"We know," Momma said quickly. "Tim's promised not to fight him here." She looked up into his eyes. "Isn't that right, Tim?"

"I'll not start a fight," he said.

"You'll not *have* a fight," she told him.

Her mother rarely stood in front of any of her husband's fights, though they certainly offended her. "Your papa's no bully," she'd explained once to Maggie. "He's a good man only trying to maintain the order."

Maggie knew that was true enough. Her papa had never started a fight himself that she knew of, though he'd never backed away from a challenge, either. But today was different, what with having a rush shipment to deliver. As they went from the light of outdoors to the dim interior of the tavern, Maggie wondered if maybe Momma doubted Papa's ability to handle the Canadian.

Jozie had taken up telling another story, this one about two sisters from up near Arcadia who talked with the dead. "They ask a question and the spirit answers by knocking. One knock to say no, two for yes, or vice versa, I'm not sure. Just started a few weeks ago, so not much more has come downstream yet." Jozie was making her way around tables and chairs. "I'm not sayin' I believe it, but I wouldn't mind a little chat with my Tom. To find out how he's doing on the other side."

There weren't many people in Dalrumple's. Two crews occupied tables at the back of the large room, while Long-fingered John and his men and the captain and crew of another boat had a table near the big-bellied stove.

Papa hadn't looked directly at the table, though Maggie was certain he knew precisely where Long-fingered John was sitting. He rarely missed any details, whether steering the boat or walking into a dimly lit tavern.

Chatter from the Canadian's table lessened, then Long-fingered John gave out a great, bellowing laugh. "And wasn't it a long, cold winter?" he asked out loud.

"But that three hundred and ninety U.S. dollars made it a lot warmer!"

A rumble of laughter came from the table, and again Maggie felt her face flush. He was taunting Papa about the fight, and from the slight hitch in her father's step, it was clear it had registered. To Maggie's amazement, Papa didn't stop to confront the Canadian.

Jozie's voice grew louder as she tried to drown out Long-fingered John, but Maggie was still able to hear him say, "Hoping for another such bonus this year."

"Don't you pay him no heed, Tim Haggarty," Jozie whispered. "He's a lout and a braggart, but the Canal Company says I have to serve him."

"There's no problem," Papa said easily, "that a pint of your finest won't put right."

Why hadn't Papa said something back, if only to show he wasn't afraid? A dismissive wave of the hand would have been enough. Papa had been moody all winter long and clearly nursing a grudge that even his drinking couldn't put right. Yet he'd taken Long-fingered John's remarks — his challenge — without comment.

They entered the taproom, and Maggie, her parents, and Uncle Hen took seats at a table, while Jozie told Walter, the barman, what to serve up.

"Walter's getting some bark tea for you," Jozie told Momma. "It's good for whatever's ailing you, Anna, and that's the truth. As for you boys, it's early in the day, but I want you to taste my newest recipe."

Walter returned with Momma's tea, then drew two glasses of ale for Papa and Hen. Maggie's was last — a pint glass of dark amber root beer.

Uncle Hen took a long, thoughtful sip. "Ah, heaven's sweet nectar," he pronounced dramatically. "Better than any Greek potion is Dalrumple's Erie Ale."

Jozie slapped his shoulder playfully and took a seat at the table, cradling a glass of her own. "Oh, you. Always kidding ol' Jozie with your fancy words." But Maggie could tell by her shy smile that Jozie appreciated the compliment.

Uncle Hen began telling about his latest trip to New York City, a journey he made every winter to visit bookshops and take in an opera or two. Hen had wanted to be a teacher, but when his mother died and his father moved away, he had to leave school to help his big brother run his boat. In a way, Maggie realized, he was as trapped as she was, though maybe his once-a-year expedition to New York let him escape.

Usually, Maggie enjoyed listening to Hen's stories, but today her thoughts wandered about — to her papa's

unusual behavior and her momma's mysterious ill-
ness, to those sneaky, nasty, rotten kids from the night
before.

Just then, there was a surprised shout from the adjoin-
ing room, followed by the crash of glasses shattering, a
thunder clap of metal, and a chorus of robust cusses.
Maggie gulped down a mouthful of root beer so quickly
that it felt like a rock going down her throat. Then she
heard Eamon's voice, ". . . You let go-a me, you . . ."

Papa was the first one out of his chair and flying
toward the shouting.

"Tim," her momma cautioned as she got up to follow.

"Lord Almighty . . ." Jozie struggled to push herself
up. "What could possibly . . ."

By the time Maggie had gotten up, Jozie was already
exiting the taproom, elbowing Uncle Hen aside as she did.

Maggie trailed along, blinking and dazed by the sudden change.

Once in the main room, she spied a knot of men
standing near the stove. One, Russell Ackroyd, was holding Eamon at arm's length while the boy wildly threw
punches. "Someone take this boy outta here," Russell
shouted, "before he hurts hisself."

"Let him loose, Russell!" Papa ordered, coming up
behind Eamon.

"Not till someone tames him down some," the man replied as he dodged a boot. He was a short, thin fellow, not even as tall as Maggie, with a long droopy mustache and sad eyes. One of Long-fingered John's men.

Papa grabbed Eamon by the back of his shirt and hauled him out of the man's grasp, depositing him safely to the side. He turned and glared at Russell.

"He attacked us!" Russell sputtered, looking up into Papa's enraged face. "Come through that door there and took out after John here, only he kicked me in the shin instead and . . . and punched my hat off. Knocked over Walter, too."

"And our drinks," Long-fingered John's driver muttered. Shards of glass and a lake of ale covered the table, several rivulets dribbling over the edge and onto the floor where Walter sat looking confused.

"He's a menace," Russell went on, waving a finger at Eamon. "You oughta teach him some manners, or . . . or someone else might have to."

"Touch my boy again," Papa said sharply, "and I'll snap your neck in two. . . ."

"Go ahead, Pa, hit him!" urged Eamon. He charged forward, but Papa blocked him with his forearm.

"Now, now, no one will hit anybody," said Jozie firmly. She'd come around Papa to separate him from the little man. "And you, Walter, why don't you stop your gawping and get to cleaning up this mess."

Walter got himself up, but did nothing other than study his ale-soaked pants and the hat he'd sat on.

"Walter!" Jozie insisted. "Sometime today will do."

"Oh, I see your game," Russell said as he picked up his crushed, dripping hat. "First you send your boy over to pick a fight, and then you wade in. Real clever."

Papa took a step toward the man, a move that froze everyone for a second in anticipation. He wouldn't hit that man, Maggie thought, alarmed. Not someone so tiny and weak-seeming.

Jozie squared herself solid to block Papa. "I said there's to be no fighting in here. And you" — she pointed at Russell — "you close that yap of yours and set down!" The man opened his mouth to protest, but Jozie cut him short with, "I said set down!"

Grumbling, Russell did as he was told. Papa stood a second before exhaling a great long breath of air. Maggie noticed then that Long-fingered John had remained seated at the table, his chair pushed back to avoid the dripping ale, a sly smile on his face.

"We should be going anyway," Papa announced. "We've still a long ways to go today." He glanced around. "Anna. Let's collect our belongings."

"Oh, don't be going on account of this little thing," Jozie said. Maggie couldn't tell if she was talking about the fight or Russell Ackroyd. "You've still some ale in the taproom."

"That's kind of you, Jozie," Momma said. "But Tim's right about having to leave. We've had our share of delays." Her eyes fell, acknowledging her own share of guilt in those delays. "But we'll stay longer next time. Maggie, go get our things while we say our good-byes outside."

"Hey, wait a second," Long-fingered John's driver sputtered. "What about our drinks? And what about Russell's hat? Was near new, and now it's not much better'n a mop rag."

Some men, Maggie thought, had about as much sense as a tree toad. Less, really. A tree toad would realize that Papa was on the verge of exploding and take itself hopping off to some safe dark hole.

Instead of the expected harsh reply, Papa only frowned. "Eamon, go to the cuddy and stay there. . . ."

"But, Pa . . ."

"Get going before I lose my temper!"

As Eamon slunk off, there were some murmurs from the men there about sparing the rod and the poor state of the country's children. Papa dug into his pocket and came out with two silver dollars.

"No, no, no," Long-fingered John said, straightening in his chair. If possible, his smile had grown even bigger. "We wouldn't think of taking your silver." He glanced around at his pals. "After all, you've already given us enough to cover the damages."

The eruption of laughter from Long-fingered John's pals echoed briefly, cruelly, and made Maggie wince. A needlepoint of sharp pain stabbed at her face where the rock had struck.

Her Papa locked eyes with Long-fingered John for a few moments, though to Maggie it felt to be a thousand slow years hauling the *Betty* against the current. Then her father broke off contact and looked down at the table. Instantly, the buzz of talking took up again and one man said, "I could use a drink 'round now," while Russell said, "I need ta find an outhouse."

Maggie still couldn't believe it, but her eyes told her it was true. Her papa tossed the silver dollars onto the table before he turned to stomp outside. "I'll get the mules," he muttered darkly as he pushed wide the door, and a blast of white daylight blinded Maggie.

Nothing. He'd done nothing, she thought as the door slammed shut.

"Maggie," her momma snapped, "stop daydreaming and get our things."

"Yes, Momma," she said as she went back to the taproom. It was there again, she realized as she hurried to leave the tavern. That prickling sense that something was terribly wrong with Papa, mixed with her own shame and embarrassment. As the tavern door closed behind her, she heard a final great roar of mocking laughter from Long-fingered John's table.

A Long Day 4

Outside the tavern, the early morning mist had almost burned off, leaving behind bright, hazy light. It was still fairly cool, but Maggie could tell it would get warmer, though probably not enough to go barefoot.

Uncle Hen had already gotten James and Issachar from the boat's stable for the next section they'd travel, while Momma and Jozie were chatting quietly. Obviously, the two women did not want to be disturbed, because when Maggie came up, they suddenly broke off talking, and Momma said, "Maggie, give Papa and Uncle Hen their caps."

"But, Momma . . ."

"Hurry along now. Papa will want to be moving. You know how he is."

Maggie complied, though a sad heaviness made her feet drag. Why were they being so secretive? Maybe both Momma and Jozie sensed something strange about Papa's exchange with Long-fingered John. He'd been meek, even deferential. Yes, they must have noticed this and were clearly worried, but that didn't mean they had to treat her like some little kid.

She gave Uncle Hen his cap, then went on board to deposit her father's cap on the end of the sweep, all the time feeling nervous. Maybe it was just because they were in Jozie's place and Papa didn't want to break the no-fighting rule.

"It's not fair!" was how Eamon greeted her when she entered the cuddy. His voice was all hurt and dismay, and Maggie found she disliked her brother more when he was like this. "They're just bullies," he whined. "So why was Papa so angry at me?"

"You embarrassed him," Maggie said without sympathy. "You're lucky this is all that happened to you."

"Shut up, you stupid, dumb —"

Maggie got her hat and left the cuddy, biting back a reply. She was too old to get into a shouting match with him, she told herself.

". . . just a girl anyways. You wouldn't know how a real canaler was supposed to —"

"Lunkheaded little dowfart!" she shouted, slamming the door to the cabin on any reply. A smile crossed her lips. The whole time they'd been at Dalrumple's, Eamon hadn't once been able to mention her being on her hands and knees in the mud.

On deck she could still hear Eamon squawking away, though his words were muffled, indistinct. The way a little brother ought to be.

"I'm almost ready here," Uncle Hen said.

"Should I hurry Papa along?" Maggie asked her uncle.

"No, I'll get him." Uncle Hen finished hooking the towline to the traces before setting off for the stable. "Need to stretch out these legs of mine some."

Maggie watched as Hen sauntered off to the stable before she went forward. Eamon complaining below, Momma and Jozie talking in hushed tones, Papa and Uncle Hen tending the mules. She had that feeling again — of not belonging.

She knew better than to approach her momma again, so instead she checked the wash to see if any clothes had dried, leaving the few that had near the cabin door. A coal barge passed, heading downstream, its driver chatting loudly with the mules. Everyone has their place, she realized. Everyone but me.

Ten minutes later, Papa and Hen returned with the second team, and there were more good-byes. Papa said very little, his face now tense and closed. He seemed even more troubled than before, and Maggie wondered if something had happened while they were gone.

After getting the *Betty* away from the shore and heading upstream again, Hen ducked back into the stable. To read and escape the Canal, Maggie thought, and maybe what he'd sensed about Papa as well.

There was very little current in this section of the Long Level, so James and Issachar had to supply all the power to get the boat up to speed. Forty-five minutes later, they came to a place where the Canal widened out with the Chittenango Feeder stream on the left. Tucked in there under a tangle of stringy willow branches was the *Bonanza*, an old packet out of Little Falls, owned by Joshua and Esther Pettijohn.

Joshua and Esther had operated the *Bonanza* for over two decades before settling into their retirement some five years back. Now they spent their days chatting up passing boats, selling baked goods to the crews — and never moving an inch.

"Hello there," Joshua called out in a booming, cheerful voice the moment he saw Maggie. He was hammering on roof shingles, but stopped long enough to wave. "Stop a while. We've fresh coffee, and Esther is making sweet buns."

"Can't this time, Mr. Pettijohn," she answered. "Have to make Buffalo in four days."

"That's a tight run alright. Stop on the return trip, then." He took a blue-checked handkerchief from his pocket to wipe sweat from his face.

They left the *Bonanza* and the Pettijohns behind and then a while later the forest gave way to recently plowed fields. This marked the end of Jozie's considerable property and, for Maggie, a welcome break from the endless trees.

A short-haul boat came along carrying a mixed cargo of lumber, pig iron, and grinding stones, and pulled by two massive white horses. The driver, a boy Eamon's age, was riding the trailing animal, his shoeless feet sticking far out to the side. "Maggie," he called. "We're going to Frankfort. Anything happening down along?"

"Hey," Maggie said as greeting. "Mrs. Pettijohn is baking up something that smells good, only we couldn't stop." He had gotten bigger over the winter, his hair darker, too, and Maggie only then recognized him. "Oh, and Abel — down past Harley's, some kids tossed rocks at us last night."

"Yeh?" Abel smiled to reveal several missing teeth. "You get that face there?"

"Yeh."

"Hope they try something on me," he replied, raising a fist. "I'll say 'hey' for ya, too."

"Their name's Herkimer," Maggie added. "Mean little buggers. Broke some windows and hit James and Issachar, too."

"Thanks," Abel called back as they moved farther apart. "Can't wait to meet'm. . . ."

That was the Canal. One quick hello after another. Hundreds every year. Yet Maggie didn't know Abel's last name despite exchanging greetings over the years. Of course, she often felt as if she didn't know her own parents, so why should she expect to know anything about others?

They passed several fields and pastures, the landscape rolling along smoothly, the mules pulling effortlessly now. The Long Level covered nearly seventy miles from Frankfort to Syracuse, the longest such stretch on the Erie Canal and the easiest by far to dig. Maggie knew this because her papa's papa had been on a work crew back in 1819. Grandpa'd begun as a common digger but was soon made a blower, setting off charges of DuPont's Blasting Powder and, unlike so many others, living to tell about it.

Maggie had no recollection of her grandfather. He'd

left the Erie in 1832, two years before she was born, moving on to other canal projects to the west. Last they'd heard, he was out in Indiana blasting for the Wabash and Erie Canal.

"Low bridge!" Papa called, and Maggie looked up to find a bridge just a hundred feet in front of her and coming on fast. "Daydreaming again?" her father asked.

Maggie ducked. "I guess, Papa," she answered. "Wondering about Grandpa, is all."

"Ah," was all her father said as the boat passed under the bridge.

Papa wasn't as dramatic a storyteller as Jozie, but he wasn't stingy with his words, either, especially after a drink or two. Ordinarily, mention of Grandpa would have prompted a recollection of him. Today, whatever Papa was thinking stayed shut up inside.

Uncle Hen came on deck, as did her mother. And Marcus the cat, too. Eamon, clearly, was to be banished for some while yet.

"Want me to drive?" Uncle Hen asked without enthusiasm.

His eyes looked strained, and he certainly didn't sound eager to drive. Maybe he was upset about Papa, too. "No rush, Uncle Hen. I'll drive us into Syracuse."

After passing through Manlius Center, another section

of woods closed around them and the old heaviness entered Maggie again, made her feet drag. The deep shadows of the forest did not help when she thought about her papa's behavior. Something was definitely eating away at him. Long-fingered John, of course, but she wondered if there might be something else besides.

A woodpecker hammered at a tree, producing a soft, hollow sound. It came to Maggie that it might be Momma that was upsetting her father, that she was sicker than had been let on. The notion that both her parents were in some way changed frightened her.

She was happy for the distraction when Uncle Hen joined her on the towpath.

"Uncle Hen?" she began tentatively.

"What?" He winced and seemed annoyed at having his thoughts interrupted.

"It's about Papa," Maggie began. "Do you think he's . . . I don't know . . . feeling okay? He seems different."

"Different?" he said. A muscle twitched in his jaw. "He's worried about the bonus, if that's what you mean." Usually, Uncle Hen would answer any question in a thoughtful way, but now his tone said he did not want to talk. "He's in a mood, Maggie. But it'll pass once we get to Buffalo. Why do you ask?"

"No reason, I guess." She shrugged. She should have taken some comfort in the idea that Papa's change was temporary, but Hen's tone hinted at deeper problems.

Buildings began to appear along the towpath — houses, mills, feed stores, storage sheds, and more — a sign that they were entering Syracuse. Several miles later they rounded a factory-lined curve and Maggie spotted the lockkeeper's shack. Four boats stood waiting to pass through the double locks there, which meant their trip wouldn't be delayed very much.

"I'll help with the locks," she said, handing the lines to her uncle.

"Fine." Her uncle nodded.

The gates to the downstream lock swung open and a boat emerged and was soon on its way south to Albany. The captain of the boat was a sickly-looking fellow with a sallow complexion and a vacant look to his eyes, as if he were sailing toward the gates of heaven and wasn't at all sure he would be allowed in.

Maggie heard Eamon's voice from below pleading to be allowed out of the cuddy. Her papa's reply was a curt "Not yet, Eamon," and when the boy continued to whine, Papa added, "Eamon, that's enough out of you now, or you'll be in there all day."

A horn blared so close by that Maggie jumped, and a red-and-blue boat pulled up behind the *Betty*. "I've a load of iced oysters and fish that got to be in Lyons tonight," the boat's captain bellowed. He leaped from his boat and stalked up the towpath toward the locks. "I aim to be through first, and anybody who says otherwise better be ready to stop me."

He passed Maggie and Uncle Hen without bothering to look at them, his jaw set, his eyes glaring. He had short-cropped, curly orange-red hair, and Maggie recognized him from Dalrumple's. He and his crew had been drinking with Long-fingered John.

He reached the head of the line. "You there," he said loudly to the boat's captain. "You have a problem with me taking my boat through first?"

"That's not right," the captain said. "There are rules. . . ."

"Never mind about rules," the orange-haired man spit out. "Get down and fight me or I'm going first." He wasn't tall like Papa, but was well muscled and had large, meaty-looking fists. He wheeled to face the first boat's driver, who was standing a few feet away with the driver of the second boat. "Either of you have anything to say?" Both drivers shook their heads and retreated several steps.

Next, the orange-haired man turned to face the rest

of the boats in line. "Anybody want to tell me I'm not going first?"

"He's right," the captain of the second boat called, "it's not fair." His deckhand agreed, as did the captain, driver, and hands of the third boat. Uncle Hen joined the chorus till Papa hissed, "Hen. Hold your tongue, man."

"If you're more than talk, get down here now!" the orange-haired man shouted. "Any one of ya. Or all of ya. My crew's ready for some fun, too." He walked up to the second boat and stared at her captain.

"You can go to blazes," that boat's captain said, but he did not move from where he stood. In fact, Maggie noticed, no one stepped forward. Not even Papa.

The orange-haired man gave a nasty laugh and began marching back to his boat. "Thought as much," he muttered sarcastically.

Uncle Hen moved to block the path, his fists clenched and ready, but Papa ordered, "Back off, Hen. I won't have a fight."

"But, Tim . . ."

"I said back off. We've a bonus to make."

Uncle Hen seemed to sag at the command as the man swept past him, brushing his shoulder hard, but not acknowledging him in any other way. Maggie opened her mouth to say something, but the words stuck there.

"Common canal trash," Momma hissed between clenched teeth, but the man ignored her.

"Let's get moving," the orange-haired man told his driver. He vaulted aboard his boat and took up a pole, as did his deckhand. The red-and-blue boat glided up and nosed in ahead of the first boat in line. When the boat passed her, Maggie saw it was named the *Tempest*.

The upstream gates swung open and the *Tempest* went in. It was only then that all of the canalers in line began chattering excitedly.

"No call for that kind of bullying," Maggie heard a deckhand say.

"Ten years back and I'da taken up his challenge," the skinny driver of the boat ahead said. "Yes, sir, I would have indeed."

The captain of that boat laughed derisively. "Ten years back and he'da still pounded ya into the ground like a fence post."

No one from the *Betty* spoke for a long time. "In a hurry and no matter anybody else," Momma said. She took Tim's glass and went into the cabin.

Papa hadn't moved. Just stared ahead blankly, his lips set in a tight straight line. Uncle Hen patted Issachar soothingly.

When it was finally their turn, Maggie moved forward listlessly to help the lockkeeper.

"You hop across, young'n," the lockkeeper told Maggie, "and grab hold of that balance beam there."

"I know, Mr. Mutcher." Maggie went to the upstream gates and used its wood frames to get to the other side of the Canal.

As the *Betty* eased its way into the lock, the keeper nodded his head in a sorrowful way at her papa. "They're a rough bunch, that crew is. Pushed ahead on the way downstream this mornin', too. With their friend . . . what's his name? The big Canadian."

"Long-fingered John," her papa said.

"Aye. That's the one. Took that John six punches to flatten some young driver that stood up to'm." The boat snugged into place and Lockkeeper Mutcher leaned his weight against the downstream balance beam to close it, while Maggie did the same on her side of the Canal. "Tried to stop'm, I did," he added, embarrassed, "but there's only so much I can do. . . ."

Most lockkeepers were old men who had been given their jobs after years of brutal work building and repairing the Canal. There was no way Mr. Mutcher could have stood up to someone like Long-fingered John.

"You did what you could," Papa replied. "No one expects any more."

The sluices on both gates opened and water rushed out. The *Betty* began sinking lower and lower as the water drained from the lock, Papa still clutching the sweep, still looking forward blankly.

In two minutes, the boat had sunk ten and a half feet and came level with the next lock. The *Betty* moved into the second lock and was soon sinking another ten and a half feet till it reached the Canal below.

"It ain't right, what those boys are doing, that Long-fingered John and them," the man added as the *Betty* made its way out of the lock. "Somebody oughta do something about them before some short-witted fool gets hurt."

Maggie saw her papa nod solemnly, then he turned his head to stare at the section of Canal that lay before him. If Papa wouldn't stop him, Maggie thought, then who on the Canal would?

Hang *Your* Warrant! 5

After they cleared the Syracuse locks, Papa allowed Eamon out of the cuddy. "Take over for Uncle Hen," Papa ordered. "And watch your mouth."

"Yes, Papa."

"Hen, you want to spell me while I go below for a bit?"

From the look on his face, Maggie could tell Eamon was itching to lash out at her, only the thought of returning to his bunk kept him silent. For her part, Maggie felt like crowing just a little about driving, though she held her tongue, too. No need to set Eamon's heart on revenge so early in the day.

When the change was made, Maggie dropped back from the mules and Eamon. Syracuse was a big city that wanted to get even bigger, she noted, looking all around at new factories going up next to old ones. Pretty soon, both sides of the Canal would be walled by impressive brick structures, one after the other.

It was fun peering through open doors into these

places, to see whole other worlds and other lives in motion. Even more fascinating were the many skinny alleys that ran between the buildings. She could pause, and for brief seconds gaze up the dark slivers and wonder if she dared run up one to see inside the mysterious city.

"Uncle Hen," she said as the *Betty* pulled even with her. She was going to ask how big Syracuse was compared to New York City when she remembered asking him about Papa earlier. Fortunately, he was still lost in his worried thoughts and didn't hear her. She bit back her question and walked along.

From her uncle's past descriptions, Maggie guessed New York to be ten times as big as Syracuse. Maybe twenty times. Ships were constantly arriving with people from all over the world. Five to ten ships a day, each with three or four hundred people.

The thought of that many people pouring out of the ships and swarming across a dock was so overwhelming it made her head swim. She would be swept along and lost in such a crush, and then what would happen to her?

"Uncle Hen," she began hesitantly, "did you ever get lost in New York?"

"Lost?" He looked at her, clearly surprised.

"It always seems so big and scary in your stories."

He walked along a few paces considering the question.

"I don't recall ever being lost," he said at last. "Sometimes it's hard to find a building number, though. It's big alright, and it never stops moving, day or night." He shrugged. "Never thought about it being scary, though. I suppose the only way to know is to visit."

The word "visit" seemed to leap out at her and it echoed several times in her mind. Was he just making a passing comment, or was it an invitation?

She'd never really considered going anywhere far away from the Canal before, even though she'd thought about escaping it a great deal. Moving with her family to a house along the Ditch or even to one of the bigger cities along the Canal — Albany, Syracuse, Rochester, and Buffalo — was one thing, but New York was something else. A giant of fascinating, unimaginable dimensions, and filled with surprises.

Exactly what those surprises might be worried Maggie. Yet now that Uncle Hen had opened the door — or at least seemed to — she found herself curiously drawn to the idea of going there. If only for a visit.

The sense of excitement stayed with her all the way through Syracuse and into the next section of farmland and countryside. She recalled several of her uncle's stories where he described a street or market, and she tried to place herself in the scenes. Even going aboard the

Betty to help Momma couldn't stop her thinking about the possibility.

"You're very quiet," Momma said.

"I was just thinking about New York City."

"Oh," was all Momma said. She was cutting up onions and cabbage for a stew.

"Uncle Hen once told us about walking —"

"Lower your voice a little," her mother suggested, nodding toward the cuddy. "Your father's resting."

"Okay. Anyway, Uncle Hen once told us about being on a street where nobody spoke English. He said it was like being in a foreign country."

"Uncle Hen can certainly spin a story," Momma said. "Course a story is different from real life. You remember he had all his money stolen once."

"I know," Maggie replied. When she was younger, Momma had visited New York City twice, once staying for almost a month with a friend. Maggie wanted to find out what she knew about the big city and its secrets. Only Momma looked annoyed, so Maggie wasn't about to ask more questions. "New York still sounds interesting," was all that she managed to say.

Momma looked up from her work to study her daughter. A very brief, very careful glance told her there was something else Maggie wanted. She frowned.

"Maggie, we've got four days and a long way to go to make the bonus or we lose the boat."

Maggie felt a twinge of annoyance, wondering why Momma didn't ask what was on her mind. Why couldn't there be a moment for her? Maggie took a deep breath. "Is Papa alright?" she asked softly.

"He's fine," Mama snapped. "He's tired is all. And worried. This haul is very important, you know."

Maggie knew this, of course. Even when not spoken about directly, the subject was always there, hovering about in the back of everybody's mind.

"How are you feeling?" Maggie studied her mother's face for clues to what might be wrong.

"Better today," Momma answered. She had looked away briefly, as if she was guilty of something, then looked directly at Maggie. "Now, don't you have chores you can do?"

Sometimes, Maggie thought, talking to Momma is like going up a dead-end stream. Maggie set about cleaning windows, mainly because it was quiet work that wouldn't disturb Papa. When she had them finished, she picked pieces of glass from the two broken panes and went to the stable to search for replacement glass.

Somewhere in the far distance, she heard the galloping of a horse that immediately set her thinking about the white horse from three years back. They had tied up outside of Spencerport when the riderless horse appeared on the far side of the pasture, running effortlessly. The *klippety, klippety, klop* of its hooves striking the ground sounded soft and weightless.

She remembered thinking the horse looked perfect, especially when it went from the shadows of the forest into full light — a sudden blaze of bright white. Free to go wherever it wanted, she had thought with some envy. Free to leave the Canal without worrying what might be lurking ahead. Maggie imagined it could run forever.

A cold tingle of dread passed through her, made her shake all over, when she realized the galloping outside had grown louder and more thunderous. Riders were approaching rapidly, something that never happened unless there was an emergency.

She poked her head out from the stable and saw four riders coming on fast. Their leader, a very heavy man who teetered from side to side in his saddle, shouted, "You there! You on the *Betty*! Stop now, do you hear?"

Eamon turned to see what all the commotion was about, but the mules walked on unconcerned. Uncle Hen looked to see who was calling, too, his body stiffening.

"Who are they?" Maggie asked when she got back to her uncle, but the noise of the horses drowned out her words.

"Stop now!" the man yelled again. "I'm Sheriff Einhornn from New Boston." Maggie saw the dull silver badge pinned to the lapel of his brown jacket. It looked ridiculously tiny on the big man's chest.

When they pulled even with the sweep, the riders slowed to match the boat's pace. One of the men was trailing a spare horse. "You Tim Haggarty?" the sheriff demanded.

"No," Uncle Hen answered stiffly. "Grab a pole," he instructed Maggie. "Eamon, we'll be stopping a while, it seems."

"Where is he?" the sheriff wanted to know. He had a round, fleshy face with dark, suspicious eyes that never wavered from Uncle Hen. "Get him on deck."

"Who wants me?" Papa asked sleepily as he and Momma came up from the cabin.

"I do," Sheriff Einhornn said. "I'm here to arrest you. . . ."

"Arrest for what?" Papa demanded.

Uncle Hen said something, too, but all Maggie heard was the word "arrest," followed by a spreading numbness that cupped the back of her brain and then shot to the tips of her fingers and toes. She pushed harder on her pole, wanting to stop the *Betty* as fast as possible so Papa could show the sheriff his mistake. What could Papa have done to have this man want to arrest him? Surely not what had happened that morning at Dalrumple's.

One of the sheriff's men rode forward to take hold of James's harness, while Sheriff Einhornn and the two others in his posse kept up with the slowing boat. Maggie noticed that the man closest to the sheriff, the one leading the spare horse, had taken out his rifle.

"No trouble now," the sheriff warned, his voice nervous. He fumbled in his coat and pulled out a piece of paper. "We're here to arrest you and Henry Haggarty for assault with intent to kill."

"What are you talking about? Henry, too?" Papa grabbed a pole and was straining to stop his boat. His face turned red and a vein pulsed in his neck. "That can't be right. When was this supposed to have happened?"

"This very day down at Jozie's. We're taking you both in to await trial."

"No such thing took place!" Momma said, pushing past Papa to stand at the edge of the boat. If her mother had been sickly recently, you would never know it by the explosive charge that suddenly entered her voice. "Words were exchanged and drinks spilt, but nothing else happened. Ask Jozie if you don't believe me."

"Anna, that will do," Papa instructed.

"You're making a big mistake, do you hear?" Momma

said even more loudly. "A big mistake, so you best be careful."

The sheriff's horse flinched and shied away from the sharp, angry words while the sheriff tugged on the reins. "No trouble now. I've a warrant here —"

"*Hang* your warrant!" she shouted. "And *hang* you, too! These men did nothing wrong!"

"Anna, I'll handle this —"

Her papa's words were cut short when the front of the boat nosed in and bumped the side of the Canal, then the rear swung in to kiss the stones as well. Papa yanked his pole out from between the boat and Canal bank a second before it was caught and splintered. "Watch what you're doing, Hen!" he shouted, dropping his pole to the deck with a clatter and leaping from the boat to inspect the damage.

The boat's loud thump, the sharp noise of the pole clattering onto the deck, and Papa's sudden movement startled the sheriff enough that he dropped the paper and pulled his pistol from its holster. The men with him all had their rifles out as well and were waving them in the general direction of the *Betty*.

"Tim!" both Hen and Momma shrieked.

"Hold it there!" the sheriff ordered, though his horse had whirled about so he was facing away from the Canal.

He twisted in his saddle. "Don't make this worse for yourself, son."

Impact with the bank had acted as a crude brake, scraping paint and gouging at the oak hull until the *Betty* came to a grinding stop a hundred feet later.

"What's this about?" Uncle Hen asked, his hands shaking. "We've done nothing to deserve this."

Sheriff Einhornn got his horse under control and dismounted, grunting softly as he bent his great bulk to retrieve the warrant. "There's a man at Dalrumple's, Russell Ackroyd. He's near dead from a beating. This one" — he waved his pistol in Papa's direction — "had words with him in the tavern. Said he'd 'ring his neck.' We've witnesses, so there's no use denying it."

Maggie came around to be with Momma. Papa was still studying the damage to his boat, his back to the sheriff.

He was just a loudmouthed runt, Maggie wanted to shout, but her tongue seemed too thick. In little more than a feeble squeak she asked, "Papa wouldn't hurt someone so small, would he, Momma?"

"Certainly not. Tim, tell this man he's wrong."

Papa inspected his boat until he was satisfied the damage was slight, then turned, his eyes going from the sheriff's face, to the pistol, and back in a flash.

"Never touched him," he stated flatly. "Though I had every right since he put his hands on my boy."

"So you did threaten him," Sheriff Einhornn said.

"This is ridiculous!" Momma screamed. "It was bar talk. You can't arrest a man for bar talk!"

"Our witnesses say you and your brother went to the stable together. That's where the man was found, along with the pipe used to bash his head in —"

"What?" Uncle Hen jumped onto the towpath with a securing rope in hand. "Tim here wouldn't need a pipe to bring down the likes of him."

"We know Mr. Haggarty's reputation with his fists," the sheriff said with some disapproval. "It's well known along the Canal. The man's face was punched in as well." He moved closer to Papa. "Let me see those knuckles of yours."

Papa hesitated. There was anger in his eyes, mixed with suspicion and frustration and, yes, fear. All this was clear to Maggie, though his hesitation lasted only the time it took to blink. He held out his hands, knuckles up.

Sheriff Einhornn held a respectful distance, but leaned over slightly for a closer look. "Those marks there. On your right hand. Look to be bruises and scratches."

Papa glanced at his own hand as if seeing it for the

first time. "They're nothing," he said. "Got them chasing kids through the woods last night. Threw rocks at my boat."

"That's true," Uncle Hen began, only the sheriff held up his hand.

"You'll be able to explain all this to Judge Bradley," the sheriff said. "Right now I've got to get you two to the jail in New Boston." Next thing Maggie knew, the sheriff had cuffed Papa's and Hen's hands in front of them.

"Papa!" Eamon shouted. Until that instant Eamon had stood mute and unmoving. The metallic grating of the cuffs closing on his father's wrists had scared him back to life.

"It's okay, Eamon. This is just a mistake that we'll set right." He faced Sheriff Einhornn. "What about my boat here? I've a shipment due in Buffalo."

"You can tie up here and get another freighter to finish the haul."

"That won't do." It was a protest, but with handcuffs on both him and Hen and surrounded by an armed posse, it was a hopeless one.

The tingling inside Maggie's head suddenly intensified, became a quavering presence that weighed nothing but felt heavy, was painless but made her want to cry out. Her eyesight went in and out of focus and the world around her began to tilt dangerously.

Momma had jumped down to the towpath and was talking urgently to Papa and the sheriff, trying to sort the situation out. Her voice was raised, but with weapons drawn she was struggling to contain her anger. No trial could be held until the circuit judge got to New Boston, the sheriff told her. Papa told her to get the shipment to Buffalo, and when her mother said that she didn't want to leave him, Papa overruled her. Then Papa asked the sheriff to send word to Jozie about their arrest and ask her to find him a good lawyer.

After this, Papa and Hen were shoved up onto the spare horse, and Sheriff Einhornn hauled himself back into his saddle, his pistol still out. All of the men started moving slowly downstream with Momma walking alongside, talking to Papa.

She'd told both Eamon and Maggie to stay with the boat, but that order was hardly needed in Maggie's case. The swiftness of it all and their helplessness had shocked her, left her momentarily paralyzed.

The strange feeling in her head began to recede. She heard a bird launch itself so forcefully from its branch that leaves shook free and floated down to the towpath.

Eamon was in the middle of saying, ". . . do that to Pa and Uncle Hen, can they?"

Hadn't both Papa and Uncle Hen been acting oddly since leaving Jozie's? she thought. Secretive and withdrawn. Was it possible . . . ?

"No!" she said loudly. The stern of the *Betty* had swung out some ten feet from the bank and she hurried to reverse the boat's slow drift. "Eamon, the mules."

James and Issachar had ambled off the towpath to nibble grass, tangling their lines in a bush. Eamon cussed as he worked the lines free, then urged the team to back out. By the time Maggie had straightened the boat, she was just able to see Papa and Uncle Hen, surrounded by the sheriff and his three men, disappearing around a turn. Momma stopped walking then and watched after the men for a very long time. All Maggie could think was that her Momma looked very small and very frail.

An Overwhelming 6 Emptiness

When Momma returned to the boat her face was white, her eyes wild.

"Eamon, get those mules moving," she barked. "We've a shipment to deliver. Maggie, check to make sure the other team is ready for the next change. The faster we get to Buffalo, the faster we can get back to your papa."

The lines were soon taut and the *Betty* began to slowly get up to speed, when a boat signaled that it intended to pass. Momma let loose a frustrated cuss, the word coming out like a shotgun blast.

"Mornin'," the man at the sweep of the passing boat called, tipping his cap. Maggie mumbled a greeting but averted her eyes, wondering if he'd seen Papa and Uncle Hen being taken downstream by the sheriff. If he knew she was related to them.

Momma's greeting was crisp and direct, but indicated that she did not want to waste time jawing. Maggie took the hint, too, biting back a flood of questions about what would happen to Papa and Uncle Hen. The moment the other boat cleared their bow, Momma said, "Let's try this again."

Once the *Betty* had reached proper speed, Momma said, "Maggie, look sharp. I want to get through Port Byron before the lockkeeper goes off duty."

Any other day and Maggie might have argued that there was no need to bark since the next change was an hour off. Any other day and Eamon would have smart-mouthed about her not acting like a real canaler. But they both knew this wasn't any other day.

Maggie went to the stable to inspect Tom and Rudy. Tom's leg seems fine, Maggie thought, as she ran her hands along his fetlocks and checked his hooves. His chest even seemed broader than when her papa had bought him. No, Tom looked strong. It was Rudy that concerned her.

He was smaller than Tom, but a small mule could be a good puller if it had heart, as Papa would say. What drew her attention was his nervous, edgy manner even standing there in his stall. His muscles rippled when she patted his flank, as if tensing in nervous anticipation. Of what? A beating? Most mules could take a beating without a flinch, but maybe Rudy was the odd exception.

She checked the oat supply, which was only a few scoops lower than in the morning. Enough for a week or so.

That was the first moment she was able to look about the stable and to her uncle's bunk. Doing boat chores, checking the mules, and thinking about routine chores had kept her mind busy and had excluded other more disturbing thoughts. Seeing the empty bunk, seeing the tiny space it took up and the rumpled blanket, an open book on the pillow, reminded her that Papa and Uncle Hen would soon be locked in a cramped jail cell. That they were gone.

Her chest shuddered at the overwhelming emptiness that surrounded her. She wanted to flee the stable and its stifling air, to be outside with Momma and Eamon. Familiar faces might help ease the awful silence.

She might have left, but hesitated as the first warm tear began to run down her cheek. With it came a terrible anger . . . at herself, at that stupid Sheriff Einhornn, at Long-fingered John and his smug little smile, at . . . The list was endless. She would have been angry with anyone who came through the stable door just then, even a complete stranger. Even a mule.

She let out a convulsive sob and leaned her head against Rudy's flank, which rippled at the touch. An image haunted her: of Uncle Hen and her papa disappearing around the bend. More tears followed. More uncontrollable sobs. No, she couldn't let Momma see her crying. Not with Momma feeling so poorly and already carrying too much of a burden.

Rudy took two tiny steps to the side, but his stall allowed little space to avoid the crying girl. When his chest heaved, Maggie stood and patted him gently, "That's okay, boy. No need for both of us to worry."

She took a deep breath and let the air out slowly, wiping at her eyes with the sleeve of her gingham dress. Keep busy, she instructed herself in a way that would have made Momma proud. Keep moving.

So she did, going on deck to gather in additional clothes that had dried. As she was doing this, they came to the next lock — number 50 — which would raise them up six feet to the next stretch of water. It would take the rest of the afternoon to reach Port Byron, and they'd have to push the mules to get there before the lockkeeper left for the day. While Momma was distracted giving Eamon instructions, Maggie slipped into the cabin without having to explain her blotchy face.

The onion skins and half cut-up onion on the table made clear that Sheriff Einhornn's arrival had interrupted Momma's preparations for supper. Maggie stored the clothes in the cuddy, then put the pot on the tiny wood stove to heat, tossing in some reserved bacon fat.

She took up the knife and went to chopping the remaining onions, adding them to the sizzling pot. The scent of cooking onions mixing with that of the bacon fat filled the tiny cabin. Cutting the onions had produced more tears, some from the stinging onion gas, some from thoughts of Papa and Uncle Hen.

When the onions were all in the pot, she cored the cabbage and began cutting the leaves into small pieces. A familiar chore that felt solid and good.

"Don't let those onions burn," Momma called from above.

"I won't, Momma."

"And remember to season before you cook the cabbage."

"Yes, Momma." The exchange, while it rankled some-what, was also comforting since it meant Momma was in charge again. This small bit of comfort also brought on a wave of guilt for Maggie. How could she find any sort of peace, no matter how slight or common, with Papa under arrest?

When the onions were cooked and seasoned, she put in the cabbage. The tightness in her chest began to loosen as the ritual of making the stew progressed.

She wished she could stay right there, cooking, until this awfulness with Papa went away.

"Maggie," came her Momma's voice, "we're coming on Camillus. Take money from the tin and get some lamb at Bauer's. Can't say I'm very hungry, but we need to eat. Four pounds will do."

Normally Momma went to the butcher's, where her critical eye could spot a bad piece of meat in an instant. "Don't you want to go?" Maggie asked.

"No, I'll stay here." She did not explain why, though Maggie was sure it was because she didn't want to answer any embarrassing questions that might come up.

"We need anything else?" Maggie asked.

"Potatoes. Some sausages for breakfast, too, if Mr. Bauer has any. Don't dawdle, though. We're traveling through and you'll have to catch up to us."

"Okay, Momma." Maggie drew out the "okay" to show she knew the routine.

"And carrots if they have'm. Make sure you take enough money."

She took the pot from the stove, plucked several coins from the tin moneybox, found the burlap sack, and went on deck. Eamon had already slowed the mules, so the boat was losing speed as they entered the town. A few moments later, Maggie tightened her grip on the coins and sack, leapt, and landed smoothly. She ran off, taking the narrow, twisting street leading to Bauer's icehouse.

"And carrots," Momma shouted after Maggie. "Did I say carrots before?"

Mr. Bauer's icehouse was down a steep hill, alongside a large pond. Most of his business came from selling fifty-pound blocks of ice to passing boats, but he had a great fondness for his wife's sausages. So he built himself a butcher shop on one side of the icehouse and soon had a second thriving business going.

"Well, hello to you," he said when Maggie entered the shop. "How was your winter?"

"Fine, Mr. Bauer," Maggie replied between breaths. Should she tell him about her papa, she wondered, worrying that relating the story and answering the resulting questions would take too long. Not to mention the embarrassment. "We need four pounds of lamb for stew, Mr. Bauer, and twenty of those small sausages. I have to hurry back before they get too far ahead." Mr. Bauer stood smiling at her, nodding patiently. "We have a load we need to get to Buffalo by the eighteenth."

"You're in luck, then, youngster. I've just cut up a lamb this day." He took a long knife in hand and headed toward the back of his shop. "Won't take but a moment."

"I need some potatoes and carrots, too."

"Potatoes are in that sack there," the butcher called over his shoulder. "No carrots, I'm afraid. Maybe some parsnips will do? They're behind the counter."

Maggie put the vegetables in the sack just as Mr. Bauer returned with the lamb and sausages. "Let's see," he said weighing the meat. "That will be fifty-two cents."

"I've got ten potatoes and six parsnips."

"Another two nickels for those," he said. "I'm surprised I don't see your momma today."

Maggie hesitated. "She's not feeling well." Which was true enough, but still felt like a lie to Maggie.

Mr. Bauer raised an eyebrow in concern. "Nothing serious, I hope."

"No," Maggie answered. "Just tired, is all."

"Well, I'm glad to hear that," the butcher said. "That will be sixty-two cents total."

Maggie handed over the coins and put the meat and other things in her sack. "And how is your father?" Mr. Bauer asked as he dropped the coins into the money drawer.

"My father?" Maggie swallowed hard and wondered how news of his arrest could have raced along the Canal so quickly.

"Yes. We heard what happened last year. Between him

and that Canadian. I hope he's" — Mr. Bauer stopped to consider the best words to use — "feeling better now."

"He is." Despite the coolness of the shop, her face felt warm. "I'll tell him you asked."

"That one and his friends stopped at Camillus yesterday on their way downstream. Loud and ordering everybody about." Mr. Bauer's face had lost all its good humor. "Drunk, I think. And showing off." He sighed, calming himself as quickly as he'd risen to anger. "Well, I hope your father is better. Say hello to your good mother for me."

"Okay, Mr. Bauer. And thanks." Maggie was out the door and running up the hill. The sprint, her churning legs, the way the arm not holding the sack had to pump extra hard was a needed release. She cut behind the feed store, the tavern, and the stables to emerge on the towpath once again.

The *Betty*, she noticed, was well along and already entering a long curve that would put it out of sight very soon. Momma certainly had James and Isaachar moving fast, probably exceeding the four-mile-per-hour speed limit. Maggie set off walking briskly, carefully avoiding the mule droppings that littered the path.

Where was he, she wondered, an image of Papa's

smiling face entering and leaving her mind before she could really hold on to it. Had they made it to New Boston yet? Were Papa and Uncle Hen in the jail?

"Don't worry about me," were the first words he'd spoken after his fight with Long-fingered John. Mumbled really, since his mouth was thick with blood. "Take more than . . . him . . . to . . . to hurt me," he'd added, even as he winced in pain.

Her papa was a tough man physically, and hard to break. She'd seen him at the sweep for hours during rain, wind, and snow. He could endure a week or so in jail easy. And Uncle Hen was no weakling, either.

When the *Betty* finally disappeared, Maggie broke into a trot. She kept this up a while before she had to slow to catch her breath. She repeated this sequence several times, gaining bit by bit on the boat.

There was a good bit of satisfaction in this. She'd catch up to the *Betty*, they'd get the load to Buffalo and collect the bonus. Then they'd come back down to New Boston and be there when Papa and Uncle Hen were released. Life would go on.

She came to the last house in Camillus, a tiny, neat place made of gray stone blocks, with window frames and the door painted bright green. The cobbler who owned it had been a slave down in Mississippi, but had escaped to the Canal and freedom where he was just another man trying to earn a living. He was sitting out front of his place now working on a pair of woman's shoes, his small-headed hammer tapping away energetically.

"Need those shoes repaired?" he asked Maggie as she approached. "Can throw a new heel on in two minutes or the work is free."

"Not today, Mr. Gillem, but thanks. I have to catch up to our boat."

"The whole world's in a hurry these days," he said, though not in a sour way like some old croakers might. "Maybe on the way down, then. I'll be here."

"Maybe," Maggie called back. "Bye."

She trotted some more, then walked. Trotted and walked. Soon the cobbler's tapping faded away. A big fish leaped and splashed in the Canal behind her and some frisky birds chirped and flew across the water. All went quiet and still after this, and her sack began to feel very heavy.

Around the bend she went. The *Betty* was nowhere in sight, having already gone around the next bend. No boats were coming toward her, and when she glanced around, the water behind was empty as well.

Even though she knew Momma and the boat were just ahead, the world seemed very big and lonely to her.

What would happen, she wondered, if I never see the boat or Momma and Eamon again? What if that Judge Bradley won't let Papa and Uncle Hen out of jail?

And if the little man with the mustache — that Russell Ackroyd — died from his beating, could Papa and Uncle Hen be charged with murder and hanged? That question was too immense to even consider. Maggie broke into a sprint and did not stop till she caught up to the *Betty*.

In the Dark 7

The journey to Port Byron was awful. Momma pushed them all day and allowed only a few stops to rest and change the mules. Dinner was eaten in shifts, one at a time, so there were always two to keep the boat moving upriver.

Maggie didn't have much of an appetite. Plus the feeling she had sitting alone in the cabin, her bowl of stew untouched and growing cold, was somehow deeper than merely feeling distanced from her family, more consuming. The emptiness was inside her, in her bones.

"We can't keep at this speed much longer," Maggie told Momma when she emerged from the cabin. The sun was beginning to set. "The mules —"

"The mules can handle it, and so can we."

"But, Momma —" It wasn't only the mules and Maggie's own tired muscles. The blaze of energy Momma had had just after Papa's arrest had slowly died as the day wore on. She was now clearly exhausted, her eyes heavy.

"We're getting through Port Byron today," her mother stated to end the conversation.

The late afternoon shadows were stretching across the Canal when the Port Byron locks finally came into view. As a boat heading downstream passed them, Momma let loose a powerful string of cusses.

Maggie peered ahead and saw six boats in line ahead of them, and what was worse, the upstream lock was encased in a clumsy wood frame, obviously closed for repairs. That meant all boats going up- and downstream had to use the same downstream lock.

As they came to the back of the line, they heard men arguing loudly.

"It's the downstream lock, so downstream boats have right of way!" a man standing near one of the balance beams shouted, answered immediately by the captain of the lead upstream boat. "By Gosh, that ain't right," he said. "We got loads to get through, too!"

The man from the downstream boat leaned on the balance beam to swing shut one gate, while the captain in the upstream boat positioned his craft to block boats from clearing the lock.

"Move that thing so I can get on with this," the man who'd closed the gate yelled.

"You'll wait all night before *I* move!" his adversary replied.

"Where's that Jeremiah?" Momma muttered angrily. Her jaws were clenched so tight she had to squeeze out the words.

Jeremiah Petes was the lockkeeper at Port Byron and normally it was his job to keep order in such situations. Only he'd left off work early, assuming the boat crews could handle things on their own.

"I could try to find Mr. Petes," Maggie suggested. The idea of running to get Mr. Petes, to be free of the boat and Momma's dark anger, was appealing. "He's partial to his ale, so he's probably at the Man Full of Trouble Saloon."

Momma was silent for a while, watching the men shouting back and forth. In the rapidly dimming light, their faces looked twisted, their fists like black mallets. The man holding the gate shut was joined by eight others from downstream boats, so it seemed they were ready to back his quest to lock through ahead of everyone else.

Momma took a deep breath and held it a second, as if drawing in all the energy she could. When she exhaled, the spent, tired look to her face had vanished, replaced by a familiar, determined expression.

"Momma?"

"Stay here," was her mother's brittle reply. She leaped from the *Betty* and stalked up the towpath. "And Eamon, pay attention to those mules and not the argument!"

"What's the matter with her?" Eamon asked in a sulk.

"She's worried."

"So am I. But I'm not biting everybody's head off for no good reason."

"Watch the mules," Maggie replied, and instantly felt she should have said something more comforting. Only what was there to say that could make any of them feel better?

Momma was already crossing the framing of the damaged lock to get to the little island that separated the upstream lock from its downstream neighbor. "Now listen here," she shouted to the nine downstream men. When they paid her no mind, she screamed, "You there! Shut up and listen!"

There was an abrupt silence that startled and frightened Maggie. As if the combined anger of the group had suddenly been turned on her momma.

If it had any effect on Momma, she did not show it. She vaulted from the construction frame to the tiny island and put one foot up on the balance beam of the open gate. "Now push that beam back open and let this man through —"

"I don't see it's any business of yours," the leader of

the downstream group said. "You oughta be tending to your wash —"

"I don't need to hear you flapping your lips, mister. I've a boat waiting and my patience is worn thin. Now open that gate before —"

"Before what?" the man shouted. "Before your cake burns in the oven?" He let loose a hearty laugh and was accompanied by a chorus of laughter from his comrades.

Oh, my, Maggie thought. Those poor men do not understand. . . .

It was an amazing and exhilarating leap, especially considering that Momma was not feeling up to snuff. One second she was there on the tiny island, the next she was sailing through the air and across the dark water, her left foot stretched out to land on the tip of the eight-inch-wide timber of the opposite balance beam. Four dizzying quick strides across that beam and the same right hand that had flattened Papa years before caught the startled leader square in the nose and sent him into the arms of the man behind him.

"Hey," a man nearby began to protest, "you've no call —"

Momma hit him, too, though he was as tall as Papa, so the punch caught him in the softest part of his big belly and left him gasping for air.

"Now it's clear it's this man's rightful turn." Momma

looked directly into the eyes of each man assembled. "And none of that downstream nonsense."

The first man Momma had punched managed to push free of the one who'd caught him and was standing on his own wobbly feet again. "Blast you," he sputtered, holding a hand to his bleeding nose. "Who do you think you are, woman? Interfering with our business . . ." He waved a balled-up fist in the air. "Why, I've half a mind —"

"I'm captaining the *Betty* just now, mister. But if you want to argue more, I'll go wake my husband and you can jaw with him about cutting ahead. I'm sure Tim Haggarty would enjoy a few words with the likes of you."

Even from where Maggie stood, even in the shadows of dusk, she could see the man gulp back the words he was about to say. Several voices from the crowd repeated Papa's name, some with astonishment, some with fear. It thrilled Maggie to see how her papa's name commanded so much respect.

"Anna Haggarty, is that you?" a woman called from the crowd of gawkers. "It's Priscilla Hobberman. Danny Hobberman's wife. Haven't seen you in a dog's age, dear."

"First trip up, Cilla," Momma replied. She'd lowered her voice to converse with the woman, and Maggie caught a slight quaver to her momma's voice as a wave of exhaustion washed over her again. "We're taking a load of stoves and plows to Buffalo. If this one here will wait his turn, that is!" She put her hands on her hips and turned to face him. "Well, what will it be?"

The man had lowered his fist by this time and set to muttering something about "pesky women" not knowing their "proper place in the world no more." There might have been more but it was lost as he shoved his way through the crowd to return to his boat. Their leader gone, the rest of the men began drifting back to their boats as well.

Momma pushed the gate open so the next upstream boat could enter the lock.

"That was mighty impressive," the captain told her as he snugged his boat into the lock. "We was heading for a thunderous tussle there and a lot of split heads."

"Just trying to make our bonus, Captain." Momma stood, arms at her side, her shoulders drooping. Not at all an imposing figure.

"Still in all," the captain said in quiet awe. "Still in all. Thank ya, Mrs. Haggarty, and tell your husband Henry Sable out of Rochester says hello."

"I will, Captain Sable," she replied. A deckhand had pushed on the sluice lever and the lock began emptying of water. Two minutes later and the upstream gates were opened and the boat proceeded on its journey.

Momma came marching back to the *Betty*.

"Horsefeathers and duck teeth, Momma, that was something!" Eamon gasped, his eyes wide. "Papa will never believe —"

"Not a word about this to your papa. He's got enough to worry about."

"Yes, Momma," he mumbled.

Momma climbed from the towpath to the deck and soon had her arm tightly around the sweep once more. She stared ahead, trying to calm her rapid breathing.

"Momma?" Maggie spoke gently.

"I know what you're thinking, Maggie," she said. "That wasn't a very ladylike thing for me to do and you're absolutely right. I don't know what got into me there."

"Well, you stopped those men fighting and got everybody locking through again. Remember, you said once that Papa only fights because there's no one else around to keep the order. That's what you did, too."

Momma exhaled loudly, somewhat sadly. "We were lucky word about the arrest hasn't spread yet. Not sure what I would have done then."

The downstream gate opened and the boat that had tried to cut ahead emerged. Momma refused to look in the boat's direction, as if the boat, captain, and crew weren't worth a moment of her time. Maggie, on the other hand, couldn't resist looking.

The captain was nowhere in sight. Probably in the cabin, Maggie thought, trying to stop his nose from bleeding and mumbling ugly things about annoying women. The man at the sweep scowled in her direction, which did not surprise Maggie.

What did get Maggie's attention was the young deckhand at the bow. After helping to keep the lines clear as the boat got up to speed, he'd turned toward her and tipped his hat politely. And maybe even smiled.

The smile — and Maggie was certain now there had been a smile — had so surprised her that she watched the boat as it crawled away from them, growing smaller and smaller.

Why had he smiled? And did he smile at her specifically? She wondered immediately if maybe he was one of those simpleminded fools who smiled at every occasion, smiled even when being handed an insult. Only he hadn't seemed so timid or teched.

The light was all but gone, but there'd been enough for Maggie to discern a certain intelligent glint to his eyes. A mischievous sparkle that made her blush and worry that her hair was sticking out every which way, as usual. Had he seen the ugly bruise on her face? How much could he make out about her in the dim light?

Whoever *he* was. He was tall and thin, wore a floppy hat with a wide brim, and moved with fluid grace. That was the full extent of her knowledge of him. And that he had a luminescent smile, not unlike Papa when he turned on the charm.

Only the nameless young man was just like everyone else who floated into and out of her life. She might not see him again for weeks, even months. This time, however, she didn't want to let him slip away so easily. She wanted to know more about him, even if it was only his first name.

The boat, she told herself. What was the name of the boat? If she knew that, she could make inquiries along the Canal.

She'd gotten only the briefest glimpse of the name painted on the back. The letter Q was in the name, that much she could recollect. The *Quiet Loon*, she tried out but dismissed as not right. The *Quaint Lady*. No, that wasn't it, either. The *Quick* . . . the *Quick City*. That was it! The *Quick City*, out of Buffalo.

It wasn't much, but it was something to hold on to while she puzzled over that smile.

The *Betty* went through the lock and was once again making progress, though the going was painfully slow in the dark. A number of folk on boats they passed thanked Momma for setting things right at the lock, and a few invited them to stop for dinner, all of which Momma declined politely.

Stopping would lead to time-consuming, embarrassing questions about Papa and Uncle Hen. Momma was smart to want to stay clear of that for as long as possible. But even Maggie knew that night packets would spread the word, and by tomorrow noon, everybody who passed them would want to know what happened.

Once clear of town, Maggie took over the driving from Eamon, who was exhausted enough that he raised only a small fuss. No use asking Momma when we'll stop for the night, Maggie told herself. We might travel all the way to Clyde before she's happy.

She wondered if Papa was alright, if he and Uncle Hen were safe in their cells. Each time she thought that word, a shiver pulsed through her as she imagined thick black bars, damp stone walls, a cold metal bed.

What was Papa thinking about? Was he worrying about them? About how they were doing? Or wondering where they were on the Canal and whether they could still make the bonus? And what did he and Uncle Hen talk about in that tiny space?

No use thinking about him, she reasoned. There was nothing she could do for him out here in the dark. Nothing at all.

Done in and About 8 to Drop

Momma kept them moving upstream late into the night, hoping to get across the Richmond Aqueduct. They hadn't reached there as nine o'clock approached, but the bindings on Maggie's boots were cutting into her ankles, her tired head swimming.

"Can't we stop now, Momma?" Eamon pleaded, his voice heavy with fatigue. He was sitting on the deck, leaning back against the stable door.

Maggie was so tired, she didn't think to say anything sarcastic to him.

Momma ignored Eamon's request, and when it was repeated a mile later, she snapped, "Can't you keep on a while longer? Once we're past the aqueduct, Clyde is only an hour or so off."

She wants to be first through the locks at Clyde tomorrow, Maggie told herself, and for good reason. After Clyde, the Canal began to rise up, over seventy feet from Clyde to Macedonville. That rise required locking through nine times, every one a single lock for both up- and downstream boats. Nine locks meant nine lines to wait on, nine chances for delays.

Just the thought of the next day's uphill walk inten- sified Maggie's weariness and made her leg muscles feel stretched and on fire. If they lived on land, none of this would be happening to them. They'd have been away from the Canal and its rough characters and that Sheriff Einhornn. This was all her parents' fault . . . an idea that was accompanied by a stinging wave of guilt.

They came to a long, straight section of the path that seemed to go on forever. Keep moving, she told herself. For Papa's sake. But when she stumbled over a fallen branch, her determination evaporated. "I'm all done in, Momma," Maggie admitted. "Feel about to drop."

Momma looked at Maggie, a long, even stare, then let loose an exasperated sigh. "We'll stop, then," she said, disgusted. "Eamon, take care of the mules."

"I'll help," Maggie offered. She went forward to toss her brother a securing line.

"Don't need your help none," Eamon grumbled, even though his legs were about to buckle.

Maggie ignored him and struggled to muscle out the heavy boarding plank. Next, she opened the stable doors and went inside to light a lamp.

"Come on, ya dumb beast," Eamon said from outside. He had unhitched Rudy and was yanking impatiently on his halter, trying to get him to move toward the gangplank. "I'd sell ya for glue if you was mine."

Rudy swung his head from side to side, then pulled it back, his nostrils flaring. Eamon snapped the whip on the mule's rump, though this didn't get the animal moving forward. Instead, Rudy's rear legs hopped sideways until his body was nearly parallel to the Canal while his head still faced up the plank.

"Go light with the whip," Maggie told him. He's feeling as angry as I am about all of this, she realized. He wants to take it out on somebody. "He's skittish."

"Leave me be," Eamon replied. He swung the whip again, but missed Rudy entirely.

"No use trying to get him up now unless you plan to carry him." Maggie slipped under her brother's outstretched arm and took the mule's halter from him. "That's okay, boy," she said quietly. Eamon might yell at her for interfering, but at least the mule wouldn't get hit again. "That's okay."

She followed Rudy as he backed away from the plank, snorting angrily.

"Could've got him aboard if ya'd just left me to it," Eamon said. "He would've listened."

A nasty reply was on the very tip of her tongue, had weight enough that Maggie could feel it. She resisted the temptation, in part because she was so tired, in part because Momma didn't need to hear them arguing. Anyway, what use would it serve? "I know you could have," she said over her shoulder. "Thought I'd hold him while you got Tom in and settled, that's all."

"Well, I could've," the boy insisted. "Gotten him inside, I mean."

"I know," she repeated. "You could have."

That seemed to calm both her brother and the mule. Maggie managed to get close enough to Rudy to stroke his neck and murmur more soothing words to him.

"That's a good boy." Her voice was a whisper, no louder than the gentle rustle of soft, new leaves. The mule stopped moving about and shaking his head and stood now patiently accepting the girl's attention.

"Alright," she said, "we can go up. There's oats there and water. And your friends, too." She nodded her head toward the boat. "Come on, boy. This way."

He balked at her first move toward the boat, but then cautiously followed her lead. There was another hesitation at the foot of the plank and another at the stable door, but eventually he ducked his head and entered, his hooves clomping loudly.

Eamon had already added oats to the feed bins and was brushing Tom, standing on a stool to reach. Uncle Hen was very particular about currying the mules after their pulls, and Maggie could see that Eamon, for all of his silly bluster, was doing the chore with care. "You're good with the mules," she added. "I'll bet you could jolly Rudy into being a great puller."

"Not hardly likely," he said, though his usual swagger was missing.

"I think you could." She took up another brush to work on Rudy.

"He's a runt. And those legs of his are no bigger than cornstalks."

Eamon was right about that, Maggie had to admit. Rudy had legs with little apparent muscle to them. "He's young yet," she tried, "and he's put on some muscle since he's been with us. He'll flesh out in time. Like you will."

Eamon grunted, which turned out to be a surprisingly friendly grunt. It wasn't that Eamon was small for his age. He was average, according to a chart in Professor James Monteith's *Popular Science Reader*. The trouble was that Papa had always towered over everybody, and Eamon was always being compared to Papa.

"Ya think?" Eamon asked quietly, trying to hide the tiny smile that appeared on his face.

"Absolutely," Maggie said. "You'll be as big as Papa someday. And Rudy will develop muscle, too. Papa would not have bought him unless he saw something good in him, right?"

"I guess."

They finished brushing the mules in a silence that made Maggie anxious. Eamon was usually either chattering about one thing or another or singing an old tune, so his quiet now was unnatural.

"You worried?" she asked. She'd begun straightening up Uncle Hen's bed. "About Papa and Uncle Hen?"

"Why should I be?" he said quickly. His eyes were suddenly very shiny and Maggie thought he might be about to cry. "They didn't do nothing to that stupid little bully, and if they did, then he deserved it!"

"Momma's worried, too, and so am I. If that man doesn't wake up . . ."

She didn't finish the sentence. Couldn't. Like the water's current, the sentence and what might happen to Papa and Hen as a result flowed along logically, could only be delayed and not stopped once in motion.

"Anyway," Maggie continued, "we need to help Momma all we can. . . ."

"We already are."

"Didn't say we weren't. But we need to do more.

To . . . to think ahead, is what we need to do. Usually Papa or Uncle Hen tells us what needs doing. Plus Momma. Now it's only Momma, so it's up to us to do some of that thinking, or we're not going to make it."

"Like what?" Eamon asked. He was sitting on the feed bin, his drooping eyes suddenly coming alert.

"Well," said Maggie, "when we finish here, all the lines on board need to be coiled neat. The poles have to be on their hooks. Things like that. And someone should check to be sure the boat's secure for the night."

Eamon's brow furrowed suspiciously until she added, "Like Papa does every night."

"Okay," he replied sleepily. Eamon got off the bin to put the brushes on the shelf.

As Maggie was leaving, Marcus skittered between her legs, meowing loudly before hopping onto Uncle Hen's bed. After sniffing carefully, he snuggled against the pillow. Without a care in the world, Maggie noted, not without envy.

When Eamon had removed the lines from Tom and Rudy, he'd dropped them carelessly to the ground where Rudy, in his panic, had kicked them about. Maggie was about to call Eamon's attention to the mess, to scold him for the added work he'd caused, but she managed not to. No need to shake the fragile peace between them.

She got the lines untangled and coiled, returning them to their pegs in the stable. After this, she circled the deck checking to make sure all equipment was in place.

Eamon came aboard, yawned loudly, then headed for the cabin. "Eamon," Maggie began when she noticed the stable door still open. She stopped herself again. He looked completely done in. "You go below and I'll close up the stable."

He stopped, turned slowly to see what his sister was talking about. "Oh," he began, but Maggie was already heading for the bow. "Sorry, I forgot," he added in a tired voice.

"No problem. I'll come below in a minute. Can you take that glass there?"

He'd done a good job of straightening up the stable, Maggie noted, considering he usually never picked up anything unless asked three or four times. The stable wouldn't pass one of Momma's inspections, but it would be fine for now.

Before extinguishing the light, she said good night to each mule by name, giving Rudy a reassuring pat besides. Outside, as she moved along the deck, she heard Eamon and Momma talking. Maggie felt a pang of dread when she realized the deeper tones of her papa's and Hen's voices were missing.

This is no time to start crying again, she told herself. An image of her papa sitting alone on a thin, stained mattress swam before her. . . . Think about something nice, something that won't remind you of him.

The next moment it was the deckhand's smile that filled her head. It *had* been for her, that smile. She was certain of it. And not merely a quick acknowledgment that his captain had been a jerk. There was more to it — a boldness that suggested some secret adventure. Like those brief glimpses of a city's inner being between buildings.

A small flash of lightning came and went in the dark sky, so far off that the rumble of thunder never reached the *Betty*. The leaves nearby rustled gently as another pulse of lightning shimmered briefly, an electric heartbeat lasting less than a second before it faded away to nothing. Still no thunder.

It was the kind of April night Papa always loved. He'd bring a chair to the cabin roof to watch the clouds rushing by overhead. "This is the best show on the Canal," he would say. "And if we're lucky, it might turn and miss us completely."

But the storm was coming, Maggie knew. She could feel it brushing against her cheeks. It was heading toward them, and there was nothing they could do to avoid it.

9 A Stormy Night

The storm swept over them during the night, shaking the *Betty* with violent cracks of thunder, the cabin coming alive with great explosions of white light. Next came the rain accompanied by angry, gusting winds. To Maggie, the drumming of the rain on the cabin sounded like a thousand rat-faced little townies pounding on the roof and screaming, "Dirty canal girl, dirty canal girl, dirty canal girl. . . ."

The heart of the storm passed quickly and soon the thunder was once again a faint rumble. The rain, however, continued without letup. Eyes closed, Maggie listened to the mix of sounds — the rapid *plink-plink-plink* of rain striking the upside-down washtub, a stream of roof water splashing somewhere on deck, the groan of heavy boat beams.

One sound she couldn't identify. A soft squeak of wood rubbing against wood. The sweep moving about maybe?

No, this squeak came from the bow section and seemed in rhythm with the boat's swaying.

The gangplank, she realized then. As the boat swayed to the movement of the water, the thick piece of wood was rubbing back and forth against the deck where it rested.

We're fine, she thought. Eamon had checked the lines carefully. Besides, she could feel the lines resisting firmly as the *Betty* tugged at them. Still, you never knew what might happen. . . . And what about Rudy? He was a nervous creature on the nicest of days, so what was he going through during such a stormy night?

Maggie lay in her bunk, her thoughts jumping from Rudy to the plank and back. Everything is okay, she reassured herself, feeling annoyed that Papa wasn't there to share her worry. Or that Momma didn't wake up to take care of things. And who worries what a silly mule is feeling anyway!

"Dang," she muttered. Blinking her eyes open, she rolled from her bunk and began fumbling her canvas jacket on over her sleeping gown. Her boots came next, though she didn't bother lacing them, followed by the wide-brimmed straw hat.

This isn't fair, she thought, shoving aside the curtain to the cuddy. Momma and Eamon get to sleep, and I'll bet even Papa and Uncle Hen are snoring away, too. She lit the storm lamp before unlatching the cabin door.

The girl's foul mood intensified when the first cold spatter of rain soaked her face and neck. No one else is out in weather like this, she thought, except me. Well, this is what you wanted, remember? To ease Momma's burden.

Maggie got the plank aboard and in place with only one little slip that pinched her fingers. She was sucking on them when she entered the stable and found Rudy standing, as if waiting for her.

"Hey," she said, patting him gently. "It's nasty out there, but at least the worst is past."

The other three mules were curled up and at rest, though Issachar's ears wiggled as she spoke. Marcus had covered his eyes from the lamplight with a paw, but in no other way stirred from his cozy spot on Uncle Hen's bunk.

She took the parsnip she'd held out of the stew from her jacket pocket and offered it to Rudy. "Here, boy. Thought you might need this. It's sweet."

Rudy sniffed suspiciously at the long, thin root, then bit off a small piece and chewed carefully. The rest of the parsnip, greens and all, he took in a series of quick, noisy bites.

Well, she realized, that was pretty silly, thinking

there'd been any sort of problem. You could have stayed warm in your bunk, except for that imagination of yours.

She was in the middle of sighing when she caught herself and stopped. Where would sighing get her anyway, she wanted to know. Nowhere is where.

She decided to finish neatening up the stable. In a way that would please her momma. Lining up Uncle Hen's books according to height, making sure all the lines and traces were not only untangled and on their pegs, but hanging neatly. She finished by shooing Marcus from Hen's bunk, then carefully stowing his blanket and pillow on their shelf.

"No you don't," she told Marcus, who was about to leap back onto the bunk. She folded the bunk up and latched it in place, something she'd resisted doing all day. Afraid it would make it seem as if Uncle Hen wouldn't be returning for a very long time.

"He'll be back," she told Marcus, "just as soon as that stupid Sheriff Einhorn sees his mistake. Could happen tomorrow even." That wasn't likely, but it felt good to hear it said out loud.

Back in the cabin, she was shaking out water from the bottom of her sleeping gown when a weary voice came from the cuddy.

"Don't forget to wipe up that water, Maggie."

Maggie flinched and felt herself scowl. Her momma had slept through the noisiest storm in history, but she could hear drops of water landing on her floor. "I will, Momma."

She had no recollection of cleaning and polishing the floor, and no recollection of going to sleep again, either. All she knew was that one second after she closed her eyes, Momma was shaking her and saying, "Wake up, Maggie. You, too, Eamon. Time to get moving." There was an unmistakable weariness to her voice, a hollowness that made her words seem far away.

Maggie opened her eyes to total darkness.

There was a rustling of a blanket from the bunk below her and a soft, confused murmuring.

"Eamon, it's time to get up," Momma said more loudly, shaking him. "No dawdling today. We've a lot to do."

"Huh?" Eamon asked. "What?"

"It's time to get up, Eamon. We need to be off."

There was more movement of his blanket and a groan as he stretched. Then he wailed, "It's not even morning, Momma! It's still night out!"

"The sun will be up soon enough. I want to get across the aqueduct and be in Clyde at the head of that line. We've no time to lose." Momma left the cuddy to fix breakfast.

"It isn't fair. . . ."

"Eamon!" Maggie snapped. She could feel the angry words about to fly from her mouth — something about shutting up, helping Momma, and not causing silly, stupid problems. Only she bit them off. "I'll get dressed first," she suggested in a quieter voice, dropping from her bunk. She worked to make her words sound casual and not the grumpy way she felt. "But don't take too long getting up."

"Huh? Oh, yeah. Okay." His left leg poked from under the blanket and wiggled about until his foot touched the floor. "I'm nearly up."

"I hope so," Maggie said. As she'd grown older and her body began to change, Maggie had perfected the skill of getting into her clothes while still wearing her sleeping gown. This often required balancing on a single foot while maneuvering one or another garment on, which was the only time the cuddy's narrow space came in handy. There was always a wall or bunk frame inches away to stop her from tumbling over.

"Eamon," she said just before leaving the cuddy.

"I'm up, I'm up," the boy responded, his other foot appearing from under the blanket. "See?"

"Is he up yet?" was Momma's greeting when Maggie came into the cabin.

"Almost."

"It's raining still and not likely to ease off. Which could work to our favor." Momma meant that a lot of boats wouldn't budge until the rain eased up some. Unless, of course, they had bonuses to make, too.

Her mother already had a skillet of sausages and cut-up potatoes sizzling on the stove, the aroma surrounding Maggie and making her mouth water. Once again, she felt a pang of guilt over enjoying something as common as the smell of breakfast cooking, though this time her hunger won out. She grabbed a hot sausage and nibbled at it.

"What do you think Papa and Uncle Hen will have for breakfast?" she asked. Something, she hoped, more than just the bread and water she'd once heard prisoners got.

Momma didn't answer her question. She didn't even reprimand Maggie for grabbing a sausage from the pan. Instead, Momma was poking aimlessly with a fork at a sausage, her eyes staring at but not really seeing what she was doing. The person who had pushed them to keep moving the day before was there, and yet not there.

"Momma?" Maggie asked. "You feeling okay?"

Her momma took a second before she looked at

Maggie. "Yes," she replied. There was another pause, and her brow creased. "What is it, Maggie?"

"Thought I'd get the mules up and fed before breakfast. So we'll be ready."

"Fine." Her mother turned back to the sausages. "Don't be long, though."

"Okay, Momma." To her brother on the other side of the curtain, Maggie added, "Are you dressed yet, Eamon?"

"Sure, sure. See?" He yawned again, struggling to stay awake. "Almost there."

The rain, Maggie noticed the moment she stepped outside, was steady, but not the pelting, big-drops downpour of the night before. The air was warmer, too. That, at least, made the wet that touched her skin less startling. It also made setting out the plank an easier task, so she was able to avoid pinching her fingers again.

Next, she got the mules up, fed, and watered, and even put harnesses on James and Issachar, along with the canvas sheets that kept rainwater from their backs and legs. Maggie's thoughts flew back to her mother, to that distracted, empty look she was wearing moments before. If she got sick again, they'd have to stop until she felt better. With only three days left, any time wasted might be the difference between getting or losing the bonus.

I'm probably making too much of it, Maggie told herself. Momma's tired and upset, is all. Yet an uneasy feeling clung to her.

"I don't want any arguments," Momma was telling Eamon as Maggie came back into the cabin. Maggie was relieved to hear some of the familiar firmness in Momma's words. "You'll drive till we get through Clyde, and then Maggie'll take over. She's got more experience passing slow boats." She looked up at Maggie. "Sit and eat quickly. I want to make Rochester today."

"Rochester?" Maggie asked.

"Rochester," Momma said without hesitation. "I'll check to make sure that storm didn't shift the load." She was up and on deck a second later.

Rochester, Maggie knew, was over forty miles and fourteen locks away. Plus they'd have to stop at the weigh station, which was just this side of the city.

"She's mad," Eamon explained, "'cause she puked and some got on the floor."

"Momma was sick?"

"Yeah. She started to eat a sausage and then she . . ." The boy shrugged and pointed to the slops bucket.

Maggie glanced toward the bucket, but quickly averted her eyes. What sort of sickness lingers for so many days? she asked herself. Something really bad, was all she could think. It didn't matter what it was since they didn't have time to stop and find a proper doctor for her anyway. In fact, there wasn't anything Maggie could think to do except make sure they reached Rochester like Momma wanted.

Forty miles and fourteen locks to Rochester. If she thought yesterday had been hard, today promised to be even worse. Maggie let out a long bottled-up sigh before trudging up the stairs to join Momma.

10 The Dark Presence

Despite the rain, despite Momma feeling poorly, they left with astonishing speed. For more than an hour they glided along, passing one sleeping boat after another and crossing the Richmond Aqueduct without encountering any slow traffic. The world, it seemed, had decided to let them sail through without a hitch. That is, until they came to Clyde.

"How many?" Momma demanded, meaning how many boats were already waiting in line.

Maggie climbed on the stable roof and squinted ahead. They were more than a half mile away, and darkness and rain made seeing difficult. Still, she could make out the shape of a packet and four heavily loaded freighters.

"Five that I can see, Momma. It's hard to tell." She didn't know why, but she added, "Sorry, Momma."

Momma didn't respond, but she did make an annoyed hissing sound, a short burst of air shot out between clenched teeth. "It's an hour lost," her mother stated as she wobbled, then reached for the stern rail to steady herself. "Maybe more in this wet."

"We can make it up later," Maggie said. "We've done it before."

Maybe it was the dim light, but there seemed to be dark circles under Momma's eyes.

"Let's hope so," Momma said wearily. "Blow the horn, and then get ready with a pole."

It was everywhere, in her mother's voice, in the way her shoulders drooped. That sudden loss of energy and hope.

"And maybe there aren't many boats heading downstream," Maggie added. She let rip a loud blast from the brass horn before Momma could respond.

There was a hint of gloomy light when they finally came up behind the packet *Archimedes*. Maggie was forward, pole in the water, when the boat's captain noticed her.

"Heard what happened to your daddy and Henry when we come up, miss," he said. He shook his head solemnly. "A shame. A terrible, real shame."

"And a stupid mistake as well, Captain Merritt," her mother called from the stern. "My Tim would never hurt such a milksop like that one. And anybody who says otherwise is a liar."

Captain Merritt looked past Maggie toward the

small but defiant shadow behind her. "Yes, ma'am," he said. "That's what I told my crew here. Didn't I, boys?"

"I'm glad to hear that, Captain," Momma replied. "You would do me a great favor if you told everyone that neither Tim nor Henry laid a hand to that man."

"We will, ma'am," the captain promised.

"Maggie," her mother said, "that looks to be Una working the locks. You come back and hold the boat in while I talk to her a minute."

"But . . ." Maggie had wanted to help with the locks so she could ask about the *Quick City*, only one look at Momma's face put a stop to that notion. "Yes, Momma."

"What's Momma doing?" Eamon wanted to know after she'd gone past.

"Talking to Una Fluke about Papa."

"Oh," was all he said.

Both Maggie and Eamon knew that lockkeepers exchanged news with every captain they locked through. Jozie spoke to scores of boat crews every week; a lockkeeper spoke to hundreds. Momma wanted to be sure the story being passed along about Papa and Hen was one she approved of.

While they chatted, Momma helped Una get the first upstream boat through. Even after Maggie and Eamon had moved the *Betty* forward, they were still too far away to hear much besides the metal clank of the gate locks and the depressing patter of rain on the cabin roof. The morning was unnervingly quiet.

"You cold?" she asked Eamon.

"No," he answered quietly, though he'd shoved his hands into his pockets.

"Are you sure? Papa's work gloves are above the feed bin. In that little cabinet."

"I'm okay," he said. There was a pause. "Thanks." Silence followed.

Maggie shifted her weight impatiently against the pole as the second downstream boat began its slow descent. She wished there was a way to magically hurry it all up, to move everything along so they could collect their bonus and get back to Papa and Hen in the snap of a finger.

Her rising anxiousness made her blood pump faster. A picture of the steam freighter she and Uncle Hen visited last year came to her. It was called the *New Wave* and had been made by a blacksmith in Schenectady.

The engine was chugging away when she and Hen had entered the room where it was housed. Wheels and belts were turning, metal was clanking, steam seeped from various joints and fittings, making the space close and damp. "Steam pressure is high," the blacksmith had explained, "and when the steam's up, she wants to run."

That's what she felt like, Maggie realized. A boiler filled with steam, wanting to go and go fast, but held in place, steam pressure building and building.

A boat slid into line behind them and Maggie felt her back stiffen. It wouldn't be long before someone saw their boat's name and said something about Papa. Momma could say anything and folks would listen, but she wasn't sure she could ever be so persuasive.

Maggie refused to turn around, hoping whoever might be there wouldn't talk to her. Instead, she studied a line of ducks paddling downstream. But what if it was the *Quick City,* and that young deckhand was just behind her? It was possible that after Port Byron, they'd delivered their load, and turned around. He might even be waiting politely for her to look in his direction. . . .

A jolt sent her flying backward, slipping on the wet deck, and bouncing off a corner of the cabin. Her pole, gripped tightly by both hands, was the only thing that saved her from toppling into the water as it got snagged on the corner of the cabin.

"Eamon!" she screamed as she clutched at the cabin roof and struggled to stand again.

The line of boats had moved, and Eamon had only done what he'd been taught to do. Move the mules forward.

Eamon glanced around when he heard her angry voice and saw Maggie's head appear above the load. "Stay awake, why don't you?" he shouted.

"At least whistle," she grumped, pushing back her hat.

There was a snicker from behind her that made her cheeks hot. She looked to see who'd laughed at her. It wasn't the *Quick City* behind them, and the deckhand who was staring at her wasn't *her* deckhand. "You can mind your own business!" she snapped.

"Yes, ma'am," the young man drawled. It was light enough by this time that Maggie saw him smirk.

Maggie wanted to flee belowdeck to hide, though she knew she couldn't. She had to stay put while the deckhand behind laughed at her clumsiness. She rammed the pole into the muck of the Canal and pushed hard to get the *Betty* back in place.

There were no other downstream boats to lock through, so it only took twenty-five minutes for it to be their turn. Twenty-five minutes that seemed an eternity to Maggie, who was convinced she heard more snickers and whispered asides from the boat behind. Worse still, with Momma right there, there was no way Maggie could ask Una about the *Quick City*. Finally, as they exited the lock, Momma climbed aboard with a grunt.

"What was that scream about?" Momma asked as she took the sweep and guided the *Betty* around a line company's anchored pay boat.

"Fell over some," Maggie answered, shrugging. "Bumped my head, too."

"Oh," Momma said. "Take over for Eamon and don't be afraid to push those mules."

"I won't, Momma." Clearly, there would be no sympathy for her bruised noggin, but at least Momma wasn't sounding so tired.

Captain Merritt's packet was already gone from view by the time the *Betty* had locked through, but they overtook one of the slow-moving freighters almost immediately. A few moments later Momma called to Maggie, "I want to pass as many boats as possible before we get to Lyons."

"Okay," Maggie answered, giving James a flick of the whip. "Just a little faster, boy. We're in a real hurry."

Only four miles of water separated Clyde from the next lock, but they were able to pass three of the freighters in that short distance. Even so, there were four boats waiting to lock through at Lock Berlin, and six at Lyons — and too many folk hanging about for her to ask any questions.

The mules were changed outside Lyons, a switch done so quickly an onlooker might have thought the *Betty* was being pursued by desperados. Maggie started Tom and Rudy off easily, even after Momma ordered that the pace be increased.

The keeper at lock 57 was new that season, so while he recalled the *Quick City*, he didn't know her crew at all. After 57, traffic bunched up, the Canal crowded with slow boats hauling logs, ash, limestone, and pig iron. The only consolation was that the rain finally stopped and the low, angry clouds lightened.

Locking through Newark took painfully long because three circus boats of the Sig Sawtelle Show had attracted a great many idlers, including Mr. Heneker, the lock tender.

"Some people have no sense," Momma grumbled as they waited. Of course, she said nothing out loud to the lockkeeper, which didn't surprise Maggie. Why yell at folk for holding up traffic and then expect them to pass along the story about Papa just the way you told it?

Instead, Momma was talking about the arrest with the lockkeeper's wife. Maggie noticed that her mother's voice did not have the iron it had when she lectured Captain Merritt earlier in the morning. A curious thought crept into Maggie's head, one that she could not shake: Was her mother worried that Papa and Hen might be guilty?

She wondered what the trial would be like, never having been inside a courtroom. There would be a judge to run it, she knew, and a jury would decide if Papa and Hen were innocent or guilty. What would a group of strangers think when they heard that Papa and Uncle Henry had been in the stable around the time when Russell Ackroyd was beaten up?

The circus boats had all gotten through and were now tied up in front of the feed and grocery store on the opposite bank. The crowd — thankfully minus Mr. Heneker — had drifted down to listen to one of the performers sing.

Maybe, Maggie speculated, Russell Ackroyd provoked the fight. He was a foolish loudmouth and stupid enough to do something that would make it impossible for Papa to back down.

But if that was so, why hadn't Papa or Uncle Hen said anything about it back at Jozie's? By leaving, they made it hard to believe they hadn't started the fight, or that the injuries weren't intended.

Suddenly, the feeling that she'd betrayed her papa came over her again. If he says he didn't hit that man, then he didn't, and that's the end to it. She only hoped that whoever Jozie hired as Papa and Hen's lawyer would be able to convince a jury of strangers of that.

It was nearly an hour before the *Betty* entered the lock, during which time Maggie studied the faces of those onshore to see who would be sympathetic jurors. The woman in a plain blue dress seemed friendly enough, and so did the older black man who was playing the guitar.

Eamon took the mules up past the lock to wait, while Momma held the stern in with a pole. Maggie was forward and so intent on putting together the perfect jury that she almost missed the chance to ask her question.

"The *Quick City*?" Mr. Heneker repeated slowly. "A deckhand. Tall, you said?"

Maggie nodded yes, wishing Mr. Heneker would keep his voice down so Momma wouldn't hear.

"Mitchell something," the lockkeeper said. "Or was it Michael?" He shook his head. "Johnny," he called to the boy who helped him with the locks. "That tall boy on the *Quick City*. The one with blond hair. Was his name Mitchell or Michael?"

"Michael, I think," the deckhand answered. "Yeah, it's Michael. He's new to the boat."

Maggie repeated the name. Michael was a good, solid name, she decided, as the *Betty* headed for Macedonville on a fast, flat section of water. And she was certain

Michael would make a good juror, even though he probably wasn't old enough to be one.

They went through rolling farmland for two miles before the newly plowed fields gave way to a tangled, wild forest. The stillness and brooding gloom of the trees began weighing down her spirit. Papa had an Irish saying that fit the way she now felt: *"Uaigneas gan ciuneas* — Solitude without peace."

To fight off the feeling, she pictured a jury pronouncing Papa *not* guilty. And when that image didn't entirely drive away the dark presence, she imagined meeting her deckhand face-to-face while stopping at a lock. She couldn't tell whether it was light or dark, warm or cold, or even what lock it was. All she saw was the way he smiled just before asking advice about caring for his mules. . . .

Her daydream went along very nicely as they came upon a rolling hillside being cleared for planting. The owner was there now, wearing a red-checked shirt that stood out against the light green spring foliage.

Maggie watched as the man struck at a branch with an ax, then wrestled to pull it loose. Abruptly, he stopped what he was doing and looked directly at Maggie, a fierce scowl hardening his face.

Maggie knew she hadn't done anything to deserve

such a sour look, so she glanced around to see if someone else was there. No one. The man had simply seen her and taken an instant dislike. That realization sent an icy shiver down her back. They don't know us, these landlocked folk. The ones who will be on her papa's jury. They don't know us or like us, and they never will.

11 Just an Ol' Sinner

The *Betty* was still moving steadily forward even though night had fallen and most other boats had tied up. They were approaching Pittsford when James stopped abruptly and refused to budge.

"Come on, James, move!" Eamon shouted. His voice was more weary than enraged, and even his flick of the whip lacked energy. In reply, James planted his hooves in the soft dirt and leaned back, bellowing a mighty *hee-haw* of refusal.

Eamon had been sharing the driving chores with Maggie since they'd gotten to the long straight sections between Newark and Macedonville, and Macedonville and Pittsford. Traffic had been sparse, so they were able to travel fast, sometimes exceeding four miles per hour. They'd covered nearly forty miles that day, so James's behavior was no surprise to Maggie.

"There's no use trying to get him moving," Maggie

told Eamon. She'd been in the stable checking on Tom and Rudy when Momma had called for her to grab a pole.

"Undo that line, Eamon," Momma commanded, "before you all go in the Canal." Both Momma and Maggie dug in their poles to slow the boat. To Maggie she asked, "Are those other two fit to pull?"

"They're done in, too, Momma. They were breathing hard for the longest time after James and Issachar took over. Wouldn't want to hurt them." She wished she could confess her own exhaustion as well, but didn't want Momma focusing her anger at her.

Her mother scowled, accenting the dark shadows under her eyes. "I suppose," Momma admitted. "Okay, let's get those mules in so we can tie up."

Momma's giving in because she's too sick to fight it, Maggie thought. And I'm too tired to worry over what stopping might mean to the boat and Papa.

The boat drifted along until it came to a peaceful stop just before a bridge. Without a word, Momma and Maggie climbed from the *Betty* and began tying her up. The quiet was unsettling, and Maggie had a feeling that someone was out there in the woods watching them.

As she went to help Eamon with the mules, she noticed the trees lining the towpath dotted with white rectangles.

She stopped to read one: No Trespassing. Violators will be prosecuted to the full extent of Monroe County law.

Maggie stared at the words. "Prosecuted to the full extent," she read again, her lips mouthing the words. That's what Sheriff Einhornn wanted to do to Papa and Uncle Hen. That's what most land folk wanted, too. She balled up her fists, shaking with the urge to rip the signs down and tear them into a thousand tiny pieces.

"Maggie," Momma said, "I'll see to supper while you and Eamon take care of the equipment. Bring me some dry beans for soaking when you're finished, will you?"

"We'll be right along, Momma," she said at last, wondering if that was how Papa felt when he had to fight. That sense that something powerful was coiled inside her, wanting to spring. It was a presence as dark and frightening as the woods around her, and something she wanted to escape.

Maggie and Eamon got the mules stabled and cared for and then joined their mother for dinner. It was an unusually quiet meal, and when they finished, everyone went into the cuddy and the lamp was extinguished.

Eamon and Momma fell asleep the moment they crawled into their bunks. She might be imagining it, but Maggie thought her momma's breathing sounded labored and peculiar. She tried to think of something else, but for some reason, an unsettling picture of the Canal thick with traffic and delays was all that came to her.

Don't worry about tomorrow and what might go wrong. Think about something good. She went back to her earlier dream about Michael. "How do you get your mules to pull so well?" she imagined him asking, and she gave him a handful of carrots.

"They respond to a little kindness," she replied. "Here. Try it." She reached to give him the carrots, and as he took them, his fingers brushed her hand. . . .

The next second an image of Papa and Hen in their tiny cell pushed all thoughts about Michael aside. Once again, a sense of empty sadness filled her as she thought about the trial and what the jury would think when they heard about Papa's "reputation with his fists," as Sheriff Einhornn had put it. But Papa had never fought anybody but bullies, so it wasn't fair that his past might come back to haunt him.

That was the way Maggie's night went. Her body tossing about in her bunk, her thoughts tossing about in her head. Good thoughts followed by dark ones. Eventually, her eyes closed and she drifted off . . . until Momma's panicked shouts made her eyes shoot open.

"Get up, you two!" Momma demanded, her feet thumping hard on the floor. "It's late." Momma was still buttoning her shirt when she hurried from the cuddy. She spit out a cuss when she saw the clock. "Maggie! Eamon! It's near eight o'clock! Grab some bread and cheese and eat while you work. I'll get the mules hitched."

The door to the cabin slammed and Momma's footsteps pounded along the deck.

It took a moment for Maggie to leave behind her uneasy dream world and enter the even more uneasy real one. She felt stiff and ached all over as she rolled from her bunk.

"Eamon, get up," Maggie said, her voice gravelly, as she started to dress.

"Hmm?"

"We're late and Momma's real mad." She slipped on clothing as quickly as the narrow space allowed. "Come on, Eamon. Wake up!" As she left, she yanked his blanket off.

"Hey!" Eamon yelped, clutching about for his covers. "I'm getting up, see?"

Maggie grabbed a hunk of bread and shoved it into her mouth as she flew up the cabin steps. They had planned to be under way by six the latest, and now it was almost eight.

Momma had already heaved the plank into position

and was entering the stable when Maggie came on deck. "Bring Tom out," Maggie suggested. "Rudy needs gentling in the morning."

"Maggie, we've no time to coddle these mules. Let's get'm out and ready so we're not stuck at the weigh station all day."

When Maggie entered the stable, her mother was getting Tom's halter ready.

Maggie patted Rudy and murmured good morning to him before getting his halter from its peg. They were in a hurry, but both Maggie and her momma were deliberate about warming the metal bit before slipping it into their mule's mouth. No need to start their morning off with an unpleasant cold jolt.

The same care was used to get Tom and Rudy out of the stable, onto the towpath, and the traces put on and cinched. A foolish mistake here could injure an animal badly.

A freighter passed them as they were attaching feedbags to the mules.

"Heard what happened, Mrs. Haggarty," the captain called as his boat, the *Syracuse Maiden*, went under the bridge. "Don't believe a word of it myself. Not when it comes to that Canadian and his pals. They tore up a place in Lenox a day ago."

Momma followed after the boat. "Is there any word about Tim and Henry?"

"No, ma'am, I'm sorry. Jozie wasn't at her place when we stopped, and Walter didn't know anything much." The captain shook his head solemnly but then his eyes widened as he remembered something. "Oh, yeah, that man. The hurt one. He was taken to New Boston for the trial. Hasn't woke up, though."

"Thank you, Captain." Momma stopped walking to stare after the *Syracuse Maiden*.

"Is there anything we can do for you, ma'am?" the captain called back.

It was meant as a polite gesture, the sort most captains would make and most folk would refuse unless they were in real trouble. That Momma herself would wave off in a second. But today, Maggie noticed, her mother hesitated a few heartbeats before saying no, as if thinking over what sort of help she might need.

That pause, hardly noticeable really, made Maggie nervous nonetheless. Everything — and when she thought that word she knew it was literally true — *everything* depended on a successful run to Buffalo. One person not able to do their job, one injured mule . . .

Maggie watched Momma closely as they sailed that morning, but saw little sign she needed help. Not while taking the final locks leading into Rochester, not while crossing the great aqueduct that spanned the Genesee River, not while explaining to every boat captain and lock-keeper about Sheriff Einhornn's terrible, stupid mistake.

It was only while waiting in line at the weigh lock that Maggie sensed something wrong again. During the long delay while boats were being weighed and fees calculated, her Momma slumped back against the stern railing. Sometimes she would inhale very slowly, as if trying to settle her stomach.

Maggie made several attempts to bring her mother back with a question or small remark, but with no success. After answering, Momma would always drift off again into her thoughts.

Maggie felt a need to do something, to be moving, and the fact that they were sitting and waiting only intensified the feeling. The urge was so strong her heart began to race. "Eamon," Maggie called, "why don't you take off those feedbags and put them away?"

Eamon looked toward Maggie, then at the mules. "They're still eating," he said.

"They've had enough for now," Maggie said loudly.

"If it's so important," Eamon snapped, "why don't you do it yourself?"

"Because you're supposed to . . ." She heard her voice

begin to rise, sensed an angry reply about to fly from her mouth. Instead, she took a deep breath and said in a calmer voice, "Remember what we talked about the other night?"

When Eamon didn't immediately respond, Maggie glanced toward Momma before adding, "About making things easier and all."

Eamon looked at Momma, who was still slumped against the stern rail. "Oh, yeah," he said, hurrying to remove the bags.

"What was that about?" her mother asked wearily as Maggie went past.

"Nothing, Momma. Everything's fine."

"While you're below," her mother added, "maybe you can get the beans going so we can have them for lunch. Not sure my stomach is up to cooking just now."

"Okay, Momma."

As Maggie set the pot of beans to boil, she was feeling moody and annoyed. Papa and Hen locked in jail and Momma sick and listless. She jabbed at the burning wood to see the sparks fly and slammed the metal door shut. Well, she wasn't about to let anything slow down the run. Not if she could help it.

The voice was raspy when she first heard it, like a dull saw being drawn across a plank. A curious blend

of an Irish-Scotch burr with some New England flinti-
ness besides. "Mrs. Haggrety, ma'am." The man cleared
his throat loudly. "Ah, good day ta ya, ma'am. Sorry ta
desturb ya. I am Billy Black and while ya do not know
me, I know about ya and yer husband and his troubles."

There was a pause and Maggie wondered if her
momma was trying to puzzle out who this Billy Black
might be and what he wanted of her.

"It is all a mistake that will be corrected, Mr. Black,"
her mother replied shortly.

"I've na doubt about that, Mrs. Haggrety. Na doubt
'tall. I'm here ta pravide my sarvices ta ya till it's all set
straight agen."

Maggie glanced out the cabin window and saw the
man, hat in hand, standing by the side of the boat. He was
of middling height with a hefty, square shape. His face
was round and flushed, with long, scraggly hair the color
of bleached bone, flapping in the breeze. It was his eyes,
though, that startled Maggie. They were small and dark,
like glistening, black pebbles, and very intense.

"Thank you for your kind offer, Mr. Black, but we
can manage on our —"

"Beggin' yer pardon, ma'am, but I think you culd use
Billy Black's help jest a little. Judgin' by the looks of
things."

"Mr. Black," Momma cut in, and Maggie felt herself tense in anticipation of the explosion to come. "Who do you think you are to talk to me like that!"

"I am no one 'tall, ma'am. No one. Just an ol' sinner doing penance as derected by the Lord. And the Lord, it was, who came to me in my dreams and told me that ya needed Billy Black, ma'am. The Lord Hisself." He paused a moment, his fingers playing nervously with the brim of his hat. He smiled to show several missing teeth. "We can't really argue with the Lord when He is so direct, now can we, Mrs. Haggrety?"

Now Incline Me 12
to Repent

A second later, Maggie was standing on the stern deck beside her mother.

"And where was this Lord of yours when they took my Tim away, Mr. Black?" Momma paused to glare at Billy Black. When the man opened his mouth to reply, she spit out, "And don't tell me about the Lord working in mysterious ways. The truth is that the Lord didn't work at all when it came to us."

"It may've been a message, Mrs. Haggrety." Billy Black's dark eyes glanced about, searching for the rest of his answer. "That is aften how He works. I myself have received such messages from tha Lord."

"From the bottom of a bottle, I'll wager."

Even with his face a natural glowing red, Maggie saw the man blush vividly. Good, she thought, hoping that now he might go away. Only he didn't. "That is all too true, ma'am. All too true. Billy Black will be tha first ta admit it and tha first ta repent those lost years. That is why I've come here ta help ya now. As a way of seekin' fergiveness in this life and salvation fer tha next."

The boat directly in front of them moved forward, which caused Rudy to shake his head nervously.

"You'll want a priest for both those things," Momma said sharply, "not us. Maggie, take up a pole."

Maggie went forward to help maneuver the boat.

"I ken be of use, ma'am. Ken handle a pole or a sweep or a mule. To free someone up fer other chores." The *Betty* inched ahead and Billy Black kept in step. "I am an ol' canaler and have been up and down this ditch many times."

"I'm certain you have, Mr. Black." Momma was concentrating on her steering and not looking at him. "But we can manage."

"I've no doubt about that, either. You and yer children look quite capable. And yer boat is solid appearin', and in good order. . . ."

"Then why do we need your help?"

Her momma didn't see this because she was still staring ahead, but Maggie did, and it frightened her. The moment Momma asked her question, Mr. Black's eyes lit up. Almost as if he'd gotten some sort of divine communication on the subject.

"Because this world is filled with wicked folk, Mrs.

Haggrety," he answered. "Sinners. Ya've seen what such folk have done ta yer own family. And there're more still prowlin' the length of tha Canal, Mrs. Haggrety, watchin' and waitin'. Many more."

Momma spun about to face Billy Black.

"I know what yer thinking, Mrs. Haggrety. How can ya be cartain I'm not one of those eager ta prey upon ya? And here is my answer. Ask tha weigh master here about Billy Black. He will tell ya honest that I was once a powerful sinner. Sabbath breaking, swearing, chewing tobacco, and drinking hard spirits were my special sins. I admit freely ta once slobberin' 'round whenever I had a dollar and even when I didn't. But no more, Mrs. Haggrety, no more. The weigh master will tell ya that Billy Black has been on the straight path fer three years now."

"Mr. Black . . ."

"And that he ken work from sunup till sundown . . ."

"Mr. Black —"

"And that he ken even handle his share of tha cooking, if that be required."

He reminded Maggie of the annoying fast-talker who once tried to sell them some awful-tasting patent medicine for one dollar. Only this Billy Black talked even faster and didn't even offer a phony guarantee. And she doubted Billy Black could be of much use to them. He was sweating profusely, and he'd only walked a little alongside the *Betty*, and talked a lot. He couldn't possibly last a day trailing after mules, not in that ancient black wool suit he was wearing.

"Mr. Black," Momma said, not loudly, but in a way that made him stop talking. "Even if we did require help, which we don't, we've no money to spare."

"No pay is asked," the man said. "My chance ta serve ya and tha Lord is tha only reward I seek."

She saw that her mother was thinking over how to answer Billy Black, a man with the appearance of a vagrant and the quicksilver tongue of a lawyer, neither of which really appealed to Maggie. "Your offer is tempting, Mr. Black," Momma said at last, "but I won't be beholden to anyone, so I am going to have to turn down your help. Maggie, take the sweep while I go below."

Maggie knew it was her mother's polite way of dismissing Billy Black and she moved quickly to follow orders. The Canal is certainly full of odd characters, she thought. There was crazy Captain Mica Randolph who started every day by singing "Pretty Miss Kitty from Syracuse City" at the top of his lungs. And Wilcox Bloom, the store owner in Tuttles, was rumored to take a bath every night.

And now there was this new one who claimed he'd been sent by the Lord to work but didn't want to be paid. Very odd indeed.

Even odder was that he hadn't taken the hint, but was still standing near the stern of their boat, hat in hand. The urge to tell him to go away was very strong for Maggie, but she worried saying anything would only start him talking again. Instead, she wrapped her arm around the sweep and watched the activity at the weigh station.

Momma was back on deck in time to steer the boat forward. She had noticed Billy Black lingering near the *Betty* but didn't acknowledge him in the least. When they advanced another boat length, so did Billy Black, and when they finally entered the building where the weigh lock was sheltered, so did he. He never approached Momma or said anything more to her. He stood with the other layabouts who liked to jaw with the weigh master over politics and the latest Canal news, which now included the arrest of Tim and Henry Haggarty.

Along with the others, Mr. Black listened respectfully as Momma launched into the defense of her husband and Uncle Henry. He even nodded in agreement at the appropriate moments. After the loaded boat had been weighed, and while the weigh master was calculating the fee, Momma said, "Eamon, I want Maggie to drive the mules through Rochester. Maggie, I want to make up all the time we've lost this morning."

"I hear you," Maggie answered. Momma probably wanted to go fast in case Billy Black decided to trail along. If he still intended to earn his salvation, Momma would make him do so at a very brisk pace.

The Canal through Rochester was thick with slow-moving local boats. The congestion meant the *Betty* never gained much speed, and every time Maggie glanced back, Billy Black was there. Once clear of Rochester, she urged the mules to go faster. Billy Black stayed with them for nearly an hour, his short legs striding along in steady fashion.

A hazy sun appeared and began drying out the towpath, creating thick, moist air. One time Maggie checked just as Billy Black swung his jacket over his shoulder and ran a shirtsleeve across his sweating brow. After this, he fell off the pace and lagged farther and farther behind.

"He's gone," Maggie called to Momma.

"His kind only listens to the voices in his head," Momma replied.

"Who's gone?" Eamon wanted to know. "And who's inside whose head?"

"It's not important," Momma said with a sigh. "You can take over the driving, Eamon."

Eamon leaped down onto the towpath with a whoop. "Who was you talking about?" he asked Maggie.

"There was a man started following us at Rochester," she told him. "Kinda teched in the head, but he's gone now."

Eamon looked back along the towpath. "You should've told me," he said, waving a fist in the air. "I'da knocked him flat if he gave us any trouble."

"He won't be bothering us again," Maggie told him as she handed him the reins and whip. Momma was once again focused on the water ahead, her eyes taking on the same sad, distant look they had before.

They were on another level section, this one just over sixty-two miles long. They should have been able to maintain a brisk pace well into the evening, but toward dusk both teams began to tire. Rudy was breathing extra hard during his final pull. When they stopped for the night, the boat was just shy of Brockport.

"Less than thirty miles today," Momma announced in a somber tone as the mules and equipment were being brought into the stable. "If we don't do better tomorrow . . ." She didn't have to say any more. If they didn't cover more territory tomorrow, they'd lose the boat. Instead she asked, "Will those mules hold out?"

"They'll do fine," Maggie said. "I'll check them after dinner."

She had a feeling that Eamon must have been thinking of Papa because in the middle of dinner he suddenly became extremely quiet and almost polite. He even volunteered to help Momma with the dishes.

Ordinarily, the sight of Momma and Eamon side by side doing a chore might leave Maggie feeling like an outsider again, but tonight it didn't bother her. She was happy that they were able to make each other feel a little better.

Maggie grabbed a lamp and hurried to the stable, needing to be alone for a while.

"It's me," she said to the mules. The air was close and humid, so she left the door ajar. "A Doctor Prescott down in Albany says that fresh air will keep all sorts of ailments away. He meant for humans, but I don't see that it can't work for you, too."

Marcus gave a jealous meow, and she scratched him under the chin.

She continued chatting as she shoveled recent droppings out the door and into the Canal and put in clean straw. Next she inspected each mule's legs and shoes, taking care to clean out pebbles that had stuck to the inside of the iron.

None of the mules had any obvious problems. Most likely their poor showing in the late afternoon was a result of the oppressively heavy air. "Thirty-some miles to Lockport, boys, and Momma's going to want to be through there by dusk. So get ready."

She began to hum a tune, but stopped after just a few notes, as a pang of sadness chilled her. It was one of her papa's favorites, the song he sang after a hard day of sailing and a long night of celebrating. Though Papa always sang it in the old language.

The last time he'd sung it was last year at the end of September, more than a month before Papa and Long-fingered John tangled. They'd all gone to sit on the roof of the cabin to relax and catch what little breeze might stir the night air. Momma had told how Maggie's grandparents met while sailing for America in 1809 and were married on board by the ship's captain. It would have been a happy story except that a fever took her father off before the ship reached Baltimore, so Momma was born fatherless.

Thinking that word — *fatherless* — took Maggie out of her recollection and back to the stable, as an empty, cold dread made her shudder. She'd always thought it the saddest thing that her mother had no memory of her father, that she'd never heard his laugh or seen his smile. But how much worse it must be to know a person for years and then have them snatched away.

Rudy's flanks shivered. "No need for you to be sad, too," Maggie whispered. "You don't need any other burdens to slow you down."

She did not want to leave the stable with this feeling of gloom clinging to her, worried it might carry over to the morning. She tried to reimagine that scene from a summer ago and how her papa had broken the gloomy spell by singing his song.

Only she couldn't hear his voice, no matter how hard she tried. Her papa did not speak Irish very much, and Momma never did, so the words did not come easily to Maggie.

"Ag triall go haonach Bhealach dom,"

she said slowly, hoping the melody would come to her.

"'S mo chos ar lar an bhothair."

She attempted several times to sing the words, but her voice always faltered. The tune was there somewhere, almost on her lips, and then she would find herself distracted and the tune would float away.

She was about to say the words again when another

tune came to her. When she realized it wasn't a memory, but someone actually singing, she went to the stable door to listen more carefully.

The song was coming from somewhere nearby, though it was hard for her to fix the location. Words came floating along next.

"Now incline me to repent," a man's gravelly voice sang. "Let me now my sins lament."

It was him! Billy Black had followed them despite being told he wasn't wanted, despite being left behind. Maggie's sadness was instantly replaced by a blazing anger — at the arrogant way he'd disregarded Momma's wishes, at the way he'd driven away her memory of Papa. Billy Black seemed to answer with his song. "Now my foul revolt deplore. Weep, believe, and sin no more. Weep, believe, and sin no more."

13 The Resurrection

Maggie waited for Billy Black to come closer, but when he didn't, she marched down the towpath to confront him. He had no right to trail after them. Not when Momma had told him in plain English that his help wasn't wanted.

If Papa or Uncle Hen had warned him off, he wouldn't have dared to follow. But with it being Momma, Eamon, and me, he thinks he can get away with it. That thought quickened Maggie's pace. Well, she told herself, he's going to learn a thing or two tonight.

A quarter mile downstream his singing suddenly disappeared, only to come drifting back again, this time from upstream behind her. When she turned to face it, the song faded to nothing again.

A night packet traveling downstream was approaching the *Betty*, the driver urging his team along in a sing-songy voice.

Could it have been this driver singing, with the breeze swirling his voice about to fool her? Maggie stepped back off the towpath and into the fringe of shrubs, where she stood as still as she could.

Three great horses in tandem, one of them a startling white, were pulling the packet, trailed by their driver, an older black man by the sound of his commands. "Pick it up there. Pick it up, Benedict. No time to loll. No time."

Maggie didn't move as the team and driver passed her. "One more hour of pulling there," the driver called. "One more hour, boys. Not much more."

No, this man's voice was rich and full, definitely not the one Maggie had heard singing. The packet glided past next, a long, sleek vessel with window curtains drawn and all lights out except for one lamp near the captain. Aside from the splash of water off the prow and someone inside coughing, not a sound came from the boat.

She stood in the dark quiet for several minutes after the packet went out of sight around a bend. The *Quick City* had entered and left her life just as rapidly, and yet that young man's smile still lingered in her thoughts. Just as Billy Black's song had lodged in her heart like a round river stone. That had not been her imagination running wild; he'd caught up to them and was somewhere close by besides.

That thought made her jump the way she would if an icy hand had touched her shoulder. She had charged out to confront the man, but now she realized she did not feel safe by herself. Back to the boat she hurried, wondering if Uncle Hen ever felt like this when he was alone in New York City.

"It's a free country," Momma said when Maggie told her Billy Black was still following them. Momma's tone said clearly that she had more important problems than a silly tagalong.

"I don't like him," Maggie stated firmly. "There's something about him. . . ." His talk of sinning and repenting made her think he was really talking about Papa and not himself. "I don't like all his preaching and such."

"He's a pest alright," Momma said. "And rude besides." She was about to add something else, but a grimace cut her words short. She took a few breaths and added, "Can you finish up in here, Maggie? I need to lie down."

Eamon caught the pained look in Momma's face. He clenched his fists and said to Maggie, "If he shows up and bothers you, I'll take care of him."

"I can take care of myself," Maggie replied, though she wasn't so sure, considering how she'd just fled the dark towpath.

As she went to sleep that night, and again when they left at six-thirty the next morning, Maggie kept telling herself that they would leave Billy Black behind. There was nothing to be afraid of. Still, she found herself glancing around all morning, half expecting Billy Black to leap out of the woods at her. And she was certain she heard his strange voice as they went through Brockport, Holley, and later Hindsburg.

What was it he'd told Momma? "We can't really argue with tha Lord when He is so direct," were his exact words, and thinking them again made Maggie wonder if maybe the Lord might indeed be trying to say something to them. That maybe Papa had brought this all on himself with his fighting . . .

Momma reemerged from her nap just after the noon hour and took control of the sweep, while Maggie spelled Eamon driving so he could eat.

Maggie's troubling thoughts about Papa still worried her. It wasn't the sort of thing she would ever suggest to her momma, though she wondered if Momma did blame Papa for their troubles. Even just a little. It had been his fight with Long-fingered John that had brought him in contact with Russell Ackroyd, and that had . . .

"Maggie, what's happening ahead there?" Momma's voice had a hint of alarm to it. "Eamon, I need you up here. Now!"

Maggie blinked and looked up the towpath to where her mother was pointing. Then Maggie saw what she should have noticed as soon as they'd entered this stretch of the Canal. A packet horse had collapsed and died on the towpath directly in front of them, and now crew members and some male passengers were preparing to haul it to the side.

The boat itself, the *Harvest Delight*, was tied up two hundred feet beyond with its roof crowded with men and women. Several children ran between the dead horse and the boat whooping like Indians.

"Eamon," Maggie said when her brother appeared, "get ready to haul in these lines and fast. I'll get James and Issachar through that tangle of folk ahead while you and Momma take the *Betty* around their boat to that next bridge."

"You don't have to be so bossy," Eamon said.

"Eamon," Momma said quietly, "do what your sister says. There's no time to squabble."

They were lucky Momma had seen the commotion when she had, since getting in the middle of all those people with the lines attached could have been a real mess. As it was, Maggie got the lines off and clear only in the nick of time.

"You can't be leavin' that thing on my land!" the

owner of the farm adjacent the towpath shouted at the captain of the *Harvest Delight*. "It'll rot away with a few days of this heat."

"The company'll collect it before then," the captain promised. "Besides, your land doesn't start for ten feet off the path."

"Nothing's going to keep the stink from trespassing on my property. . . ."

Maggie wished there was time to stop, since the back-and-forth jawing might make for an entertaining little show. Even the notion of a halt sounded appealing. They hadn't rested at all that morning, not even to pee, and now she had a pebble in her boot.

She came to the knot of people on the towpath, glad she didn't have to lead a nervous Rudy through. Not with the two men still arguing loudly, the other men cussing and encouraging each other as they pushed and dragged the carcass along, kids dashing about and screaming.

She spotted Billy Black the moment she got the mules past the dead horse. He was standing to the side, his hands behind his back. Like some dark angel there to remind them of their sins. The moment she recognized him, he looked up at her and nodded his head, tipping his hat in a slow, graceful "at your service" sort of motion.

Maggie winced, averted her eyes, and hurried James

and Issachar along, all thoughts of stopping forgotten. The sooner they were moving again, the sooner they would lose the annoying Mr. Black. A few steps later, she glanced back at him, only to see he was no longer paying attention to her. Instead, he had pushed through the swarm of men surrounding the horse. Several of them objected to his getting in the way, but he ignored them and placed his hand flat on the horse's still chest.

"What are you doing?" one of the crew barked at Billy Black. "He's stone-cold dead."

That was when Billy Black's hand flew up, formed a tight fist, and came down hard on the horse's side. Not once, but three times in rapid succession. *Pow. Pow. Pow.*

"Are you crazy?" the crew member yelled, a sentiment echoed by many of the other men. Another crew member grabbed Billy Black's arms before he could swing again and began hauling him away from the carcass while all the men started cussing at him loudly.

At that moment, the horse's right rear leg twitched and kicked out, sending one of the gentlemen passengers sailing back through the air to land in a mud puddle. The agitated chatter of the spectators stopped immediately while everyone stood back to watch. One after another of the horse's legs began to tremble and move. Next, the animal's eyes fluttered open and the head tossed about wildly. With a great snort, the horse struggled to rise.

"Oh, my Lord," the captain whispered, pulling off his cap as if he'd entered a church.

The man holding Billy Black's arm let go and stepped clear of him, his eyes wide with fear.

Maggie had never seen so many men standing in stunned silence with their mouths open. From behind her, she heard someone on the roof of the packet shriek, followed by a collective gasp from the crowd as the horse heaved itself clumsily to its feet. The beast staggered a step or two, then stood still quivering, mouth hanging open, huffing and snuffling. As if it had just completed a long, hard journey.

"Tha's okay, boy," Billy Black said to the horse. "You was jest tuckered out, wasn't ya?" He grabbed hold of the horse's mane but glanced at the man nearest him. "Ya might want to get a rope over him afore he takes off."

"How did you do that?" the captain asked. "He was dead. I felt his chest myself."

"Me, too," added a crew member.

"Creature's not dead till tha Lord says so," Billy Black replied casually.

But he had to have done something, Maggie knew. In

the way he touched the horse . . . The notion that Billy Black might have some sort of special powers alarmed Maggie, and she slapped Issachar on the rump to speed him along toward the *Betty*. From the packet behind, she heard an excited passenger say, "It was like that Bible story. Where Jesus raised up the dead man. Only I don't suppose Jesus had to pound on the man to bring him to life."

"Throw me the line," Maggie called to Eamon when she reached their boat. "We should make Albion in an hour. When we do, we can get oats and change teams."

"What's all the commotion about?" Momma asked. She and Eamon had been busy maneuvering the *Betty* with their backs to the resurrection scene, though they had heard the collective gasp of the crowd and knew something unusual had taken place.

"It was *him*," Maggie said. "That Billy Black. He brought the horse back to life somehow." She gulped, recalling the way the horse came kicking alive. "Do you suppose it was a trick?"

"Did he use magic?" Eamon wanted to know. "Did he talk to it when it was dead?"

"No, he just punched it," Maggie replied, though an unsettling recollection came to her of Jozie's story about the two sisters rapping on a table to talk with spirits. Maggie got the lines secured and had James and Issachar in motion again. She was so distracted by what had happened that she clean forgot to take the pebble from her boot, and now it pinched at her heel.

"He's just an old fool," Momma said. "No need to work yourself up so much."

"I still think he's up to something, Momma. Why else would he follow us when we told him we didn't want his help?"

"I don't know, but let's hope his new friends there will distract him enough that he forgets us." Momma leaned back against the railing. "Maggie, why don't you take the sweep and let Eamon drive. I need to get out of this sun a spell."

Eamon was delighted with the chance to drive and leaped eagerly from the deck to take the reins. Maggie moved with less enthusiasm. If it was really only the sun bothering Momma, she could put on her bonnet. Her concern grew when Momma gave her the sweep and said before going below, "Give me a shout when we're past the Akorchard."

The Akorchard Feeder was over ten miles away, so Maggie would have to run the boat for three hours. She had steered the boat before, but only for ten- or twenty-minute stretches. A lot could happen in three hours, and she only hoped she'd know how to handle whatever came up.

She glanced over her shoulder to the crowd on the towpath. The miracle of bringing a horse back to life wouldn't warrant too much celebrating, especially if Billy Black had given up hard drink. So he could easily begin following them again in fifteen minutes or so.

"Eamon, I've a penny for you when we get to Albion."

"Really?" For an instant, his old suspiciousness resurfaced. "What do I have to do?"

"Get us to Albion before that Billy Black gets there. He gives me the creeps."

Eamon looked back down the towpath to the crowd, then to Maggie. "He doesn't scare me none," he said, "but if getting there fast gets me a penny . . ." He turned without finishing his sentence and flicked the whip.

Maggie's legs trembled as the boat's speed increased. Why was it, she wondered, that she didn't think they'd ever outrun the likes of Billy Black?

An Awful Mess 14

Maggie spotted his squat figure outside of Middle Port on a winding section of the Canal. Billy Black was a half mile ahead of them and marching resolutely upstream, his jacket once more thrown over his shoulder.

How had he done it? she wondered. What sort of magic power had gotten him past them without being noticed? Of course. It was obvious. He must have gotten a ride on the *Harvest Delight* as reward for saving their horse, and that boat had probably passed them while she was busy changing teams at Albion. Maggie felt a cuss coming on, but held it in because Momma had just come on deck and wouldn't approve.

"What's the matter?" Momma asked. "You look like you're going to spit."

"Nothing's wrong," Maggie answered. If possible, Momma looked even sicker than before, her face a pasty white. "Nothing, really."

Momma shielded her eyes to squint up-canal. It took

a while, but eventually she saw Billy Black, too. "Humph."
The sound expressed annoyance tinged with a degree
of admiration. "You have to admit he's a determined
little cuss."

"I don't like him," Maggie grumbled under her breath.
"He's bad luck."

"Not for that horse, he wasn't," Momma reminded
her. She had no intention of dwelling on Billy Black anymore because she added, "Did you have trouble getting
the oats on board? I'm sorry I wasn't any help."

"You needed to rest." Maggie sighed, thinking she
could use a nap herself. "Anyway, a man at the store
carried it on board and left it next to the bin. I tried to
give him a dime for his help but he wouldn't take it."

"That's good that you tried," said Momma.

By now, they gained enough on Billy Black that
Maggie could see a big splotch of sweat staining the
back of his shirt. It seemed to her, too, that he was
listing to the right, as if favoring that leg.

"I plumb don't like him," she muttered.

"What?" Momma said. She'd drifted off again into
her thoughts, and now shook her head alert, followed
by a sigh that suggested weary frustration. "Here, let me
take the sweep. Maybe that'll keep me alert."

Maggie surrendered control of the boat and went off

to tend James and Issachar. They had changed teams so quickly, she hadn't had time to do much more than get them inside and watered. Now she wanted to finish up the job properly. As she neared the door, Eamon and the mules were coming even with Billy Black. The moment they did, the man spun about to face the *Betty*.

The quickness of the move startled Maggie, made her duck inside the stable. Like some fugitive. She never looked him in the eye, but she still noticed the sweat glistening on his forehead, drops sliding down his rosy cheeks.

"Good mornin' ta ya, Mrs. Haggrety," she heard him say, his breathing hard. "Is there any way I ken be of assistance taday?"

"I believe we've discussed this already," was her momma's response.

"May tha Lord look over ya and yars, Mrs. Haggrety."

"Thank you, sir, and good day to you."

Why didn't Momma just tell him flat out to stop following them?

Maggie spent the next half hour taking care of the mules, all the while imagining herself telling Billy Black to leave her family alone. By the time she finished with the mules, sweat was making her dress cling to her body, so she decided to walk a while to cool off. She was relieved when she found Billy Black gone.

It felt good to be walking on the path again, stretching her legs, and occasionally leaping over fresh mule droppings. The recently turned fields gave off a rich, earthy aroma broken in places by a series of distinct smells — of wild onions, sweet spring blossoms, damp straw.

Any other year and she would stroll along enjoying the sun and smells, and maybe even letting her mind wander away from the Canal to some exotic, imagined spot. But today her thoughts always came back to Papa and Uncle Hen, and the fact that they had to make Buffalo by noon on the eighteenth. Tomorrow. But how would they ever be able to do this? Middle Port was twelve miles from Lockport, and Lockport was thirty-one miles from Buffalo. That meant they were . . .

She found a stick and quickly scratched the two numbers in the dirt, one on top of the other. They were forty-three miles from the bonus, if she'd added correctly.

When she looked up from her figures, she saw that the *Betty* had moved ahead by several hundred feet. Instinctively, she glanced around to see if Billy Black was gaining on them again. A foolish notion, she knew, since they had left him behind long ago, and there was no way he could be close. Unless, of course, he'd caught another ride.

Maggie scurried in a panic to the *Betty*. By the time she caught up, she had worked herself into a frenzy — at

Billy Black for being a pest, and at herself for being so scared of him.

The boy from the *Quick City*, Michael, came to mind again as she pictured that first and only time she'd ever seen him — a tall, graceful shadow sailing past and into the night. There was so much she wanted to know about him. The color of his eyes, for instance. Where did he come from? How old was he? What he was like when not working a boat. She realized she didn't know very much at all about him.

Why had she been so drawn to him? she wondered. Why had his smile lodged so firmly in her mind? He was a welcome distraction from the problems she and her family were facing, but was there more to it than that?

The instant she looked up, she noticed Tom. "Eamon, has Tom been walking like that for long?"

"Like what?" he asked, yawning.

Her first thought was that everybody was in a fog of exhaustion and that they were lucky something truly terrible hadn't happened to the boat or mules. "Don't you see? He's got a hitch to his walk." She ran ahead of Eamon to Tom. "Momma, we're going to have to stop so I can check Tom."

"I don't see anything," Eamon said.

She remembered Papa asking about Tom's leg and wondered if maybe she had missed something when she'd inspected the animal. "His front left. He's not stepping down on it the same as the others."

Eamon ducked behind Rudy for a better view. "I still don't see it."

"It's only slight."

"I don't see anything, either, Maggie." Her mother was shading her eyes against the sun's glare. "Well, let's not waste time talking. Get the lines off and the boat stopped so Maggie can look at him proper."

As they were slowing the boat, a packet raced past them, sending out a wave that slapped and rocked the *Betty*. The captain of the packet tipped his cap to Maggie, and several people on the roof waved as well. Maggie gave them a quick nod in response. They seemed like a nice bunch, Maggie thought. Maybe some of them would be on Papa's jury.

When the boat was secured, Maggie went to Tom. "Now let's look at that hoof," she murmured. She stroked his neck several times before going to work.

The moment the lines had come off, Tom had stopped walking. Hadn't even wandered to the side to test the grass there, a sure sign that something was bothering him. Maggie knelt on the ground and studied his left knee and foreleg for an injury.

"How about your hoof, then," she said softly. She picked the hoof up and placed it across her knee so she could inspect it carefully. "Ummm," she murmured when she saw the jagged piece of metal wedged between the iron horseshoe and sole of the hoof.

"That's got to hurt," she told him, pushing the metal with her finger. It was imbedded too deeply and didn't budge. "Hold still now," she said. "I'll try to be as gentle as I can."

She took out her pocketknife and placed the blade under the metal, using her index finger as a fulcrum. Gingerly, she rocked the knife up and down until the metal began to loosen. "That's okay, that's okay," she whispered when Tom's leg twitched. "Just a few . . . more . . . wiggles . . ." The metal popped out.

"How's that feel?" she asked Tom. "Better?"

The mule tried to pull its leg free, but Maggie held tight until she saw dark red blood appear. Not much. Just a drop or two. "That went deep," she said, tossing the metal into the Canal.

"Is he okay?" Momma wanted to know.

"I pulled a piece of metal out and drew a little blood. We'll need to soak his hoof."

Her Momma's expression showed she knew that

would mean more than a simple delay to change teams. It could take a day or even two to make sure an infection didn't set in, during which time James and Issachar would have to do all the pulling. That meant a much slower pace and more rest stops. "I don't think it's bad at all, Momma. It was in the toe, and we caught it before the metal got worked in too deep."

"Well, that's something," Momma said, though clearly she didn't think it was much of anything. "Did you get all of it out?"

"I think so. But I'm going to check it again when he's inside."

Eamon had heaved the boarding plank into position and was now leading Rudy toward it. "Don't you give me no trouble," he warned the mule.

"Eamon . . ." Maggie said, drawing out the end of his name so it hung lightly in the air.

"It's okay. I'm being gentle with him," he said. "Gave him a sugar cube so he'd forget that other time."

Maggie got Tom inside the stable, then helped Eamon hitch up James and Issachar. Next Maggie got out a pail and filled it halfway with warm water from the kettle, adding a handful of Dr. Stiesle's Horse Salts.

Marcus was lounging on a shelf, watching her work. "Says on the jar," Maggie told the cat, "that it's guaranteed to cure dry, cracked hoofs, abscesses, bruises, thrush, and the gravels. I suppose it'll work on a nail poke, too."

At first, Tom balked at putting his foot in the pail, and when she finally got him to obey he took it out almost immediately. After it happened a second time, Maggie wound a cloth around the mule's leg and tied both ends to the pail. To take the mule's mind off its clumsy boot, she added oats to his trough and gave him an apple.

When she was finished with this, she set about tidying up the stable. They had been pushing forward so relentlessly that she'd let the straightening go and now her eyes found chaos everywhere. She thought about the burden her momma must carry if she always saw the world this way. Always something to pick up, dust, mend, or put in its particular place.

And then, Maggie realized, there were the things that broke down or went wrong. Storms blew in, mules went lame, loans came due, people got sick, strangers trailed after them. There was Papa, too. He only had fights to maintain order on the Canal, but that was what landed them all in their present troubles.

The full weight of the problems hadn't settled on Maggie until that moment. It felt unfair to Maggie to have to carry the burdens of an adult, but she didn't have much choice about it. Not with Papa and Hen gone and

Momma sick. She wasn't even sure what she should do, other than to work hard and hope for the best. It was almost too exhausting to even think about it.

After getting the stable into proper shape, Maggie decided to empty the one hundred pounds of oats into the bin. Usually Papa or Hen handled the heavy loads, so the fact that she couldn't lift the sack straight up was a shock. Instead, she had to transfer the oats a scoop at a time until the sack was empty.

Sweat was dripping from her, and when she finally finished, her face was powdered with oat dust. This was just one sack, she reminded herself. How on earth are we going to unload a hundred and twenty-five stoves and eighty-five plows when we finally do get to Tucker's?

On deck, Maggie sucked in fresh air to rid her lungs of the oat dust. James and Issachar were pulling at a decent enough speed. Not the whirlwind pace Momma had insisted on the past few days, but steady enough. Only she didn't like the way James's ears were lying back, a sign that he was tiring.

She was pretty sure he could make it to Lockport and maybe even a little beyond. But could the mule make it all the way to Buffalo? She considered teaming Issachar with Rudy, but rejected the idea immediately. It took weeks before a new pair got accustomed to each other's pace and ways before they could pull safely at full speed.

There was only one thing she could think to do. Despite the danger, she would work Tom as soon as possible. She would be risking Tom's foot becoming infected, which could mean days of recovery. Or worse, he could die. But the bonus was too important and time too short not to take that chance.

She could tell by the slant of the sun that two hours had passed since she'd gone into the stable. "Momma," she said. "It's time to rest the mules."

"Already?" Momma replied. She squinted at the sun to judge the time.

"It's a couple of hours at least. We need to be extra careful with them. James especially. There's a piece of open grass just ahead."

"I guess." It seemed like a real effort for her to say those two words. "I could use a breather, too. Eamon, we're stopping at that grassy spot up ahead."

The boat was brought to a halt after which Maggie took out Rudy to tether him with James and Issachar in the open area. She wanted to throw herself down on the new grass and enjoy the sun on her face, to rest her tired feet, but she had to change the water in Tom's pail-boot.

It was only after reattaching the pail to his leg that she sensed the quiet. "Momma," she said, poking her head from the stable, "have any boats gone by lately? There should be a fair amount of traffic heading downstream."

Momma searched the Canal ahead. "I wonder if anything's happened."

A while later, they were going again and it took some time before a boat approached from the opposite direction, a slow-moving vessel loaded with potash.

"Captain," Momma called out. "We haven't seen any boats for an hour. Is there a problem ahead?"

The man shook his head mournfully. "The downstream lock's closed to repair winter damage and then some drunk fool rammed a gate and smashed the upstream lock. We was just ahead of'm, the last out of Lockport. We stopped a while to help." He made a sound to indicate his disgust. "A hundred boats backed up and waiting. It's an awful mess up there, ma'am. An awful big mess."

Working a Miracle 15

"**M**ary in heaven preserve us," Momma whispered when they finally came to the last boat waiting to get through Lockport. The line of colorful packets and freighters stretched out in front of them, winding around the turn to disappear behind the steep hills lining the Canal. They were so far away that they couldn't even see the locks.

Maggie was at the sweep when the *Betty* halted behind a red-and-black packet, its roof swarming with impatient passengers. She had already counted twenty-six boats to the turn. Most of them were tied up, anticipating a long delay. "We might as well tie up, too," Maggie said. "I'll go see what's happening." Somewhere in the back of her brain a little voice was saying, "It's over now. You tried, but there's no way to make the bonus. . . ."

Momma was staring at the unmoving line ahead with tired eyes. Her inner voice was probably saying the same thing as Maggie's.

"I should go," Eamon called out. "I can run faster

than you, so I can get there and back and tell you what's happening."

"Eamon . . ." Momma warned.

"That's okay, Momma. Eamon's right." What difference did it make who went first? "Eamon, why don't you tie up on that tree there before taking a look." She tossed the stern line to him, then went to get the bowline ready. There were no trees handy to the front of the boat, so a wood stake would have to do. "Ask how long before the locks reopen," Maggie told her brother as she hammered in the stake. "And when you come back, count the boats in front of us."

"Okay," Eamon said, running off eagerly.

When he was out of earshot, Momma said, "I don't see how we'll make Buffalo in time. Not with all these boats in front of us."

Maggie wanted to reassure her momma, to say there was still a chance, especially if they traveled through the night. But the reality was sitting motionless in front of her. Probably fifty-some boats on this side, and another fifty above the locks.

Momma began talking about the arrest to the captain of a boat that had pulled in behind them. The words were the same she'd said many times before, though there was a hollowness to them now, her confidence gone along with her energy.

Eamon returned ten minutes later out of breath from running. "Forty-three boats from the locks to here. It's a real mess. That boat crashed through two gates."

Forty-three was certainly better than fifty, Maggie thought. Not by a lot, but a little better. She began walking toward the locks. "How long before they open?"

"Some said it might open later tonight. 'Round nine or ten, but that was a guess."

The moment Maggie rounded the bend she saw that Eamon had been right. It was an unholy mess. Lockport had a double flight of five locks to carry boats up and down a sixty-five-foot rise in the Canal. The downstream locks were partly encased in wooden scaffolds with piles of lumber nearby to repair ice damage. Next to them on the right, Maggie could see the gates to the two bottom upstream locks in splinters, crushed by the runaway boat. What looked like a small army of men was hauling a shattered gate from its hinges as Maggie approached.

A friend of her parents, Captain Enos Throop, told her what he knew about the accident. Seems the captain and crew of the *Northern Light* were roaring drunk when they bullied the lockkeeper to let them enter the upper lock. They managed to navigate the first three locks without incident, but at the fourth something went wrong.

"They was arguing about something when they poled into the lock and pushed too hard, then set to arguing some more. Didn't even try to slow the" — he swallowed a cuss when he remembered he was talking to a young lady — "the boat. Hit the gates square on and hard enough to go through. The rush of escaping water carried the boat over the edge into the next lock and through those gates." Captain Throop shook his head, clearly angry. "Crushed the leg of one man enough he'll probably lose it. The captain was knocked senseless — not that the fool ever had much sense."

The boat had been stoved in the accident and sunk just beyond the gate, so the first hours after were spent unloading cargo and hauling the boat to shore. It sat there now, leaning over sadly, one deck under water and every window shattered.

The good news, if that is what it could be called, was that the gate hinges had withstood the impact. One had been bent a little and could be straightened. A snapped-off hinge would require setting a new one in mortar, which could take a day or two to dry.

The plan, Maggie soon learned as she continued toward the base of the locks, was simple. Gates from the downstream locks were going to be transferred to the upstream locks. Already men from several boat crews were poised to lift a massive gate and haul it over once the blacksmith had hammered the hinge back straight.

Many of the people she encountered during her walk knew Maggie and a few were good friends of her family. Almost everyone asked after Papa and Uncle Hen, and Maggie was glad she'd listened carefully to what her momma had said. She found herself using the exact phrases Momma had used and was surprised to find her voice growing more confident each time she told the story.

The atmosphere at the locks was a confusing blend of carnival and work site, with several men shouting orders, while a large crowd lingered about watching what was taking place and chatting. All accompanied by the sharp rap of the blacksmith's hammer on the bent hinge.

The tavern up the hill from the lockkeeper's shack had several boys moving through the crowd hawking beer that was ladled from metal pails into communal glasses. A woman with her hair tied up in a tight knot had set up a grill and was cooking German sausages.

Nearby, several well-dressed men and women from a packet stood to the side of the path, examining the old wood buildings that dotted the hills surrounding the locks. "A good fire would do this town wonders," one of the men commented loudly to the amusement of his friends. Maggie took an instant dislike to the entire group.

Maggie was halfway up the incline when the first gate was heaved up from the downstream lock to a chorus of shouts. The boatmen were so anxious to be going again that additional volunteers were already tugging a second gate from its hinges.

If nothing went wrong, Maggie thought, turning to head back to the boat, they might have the gates in place well before nine o'clock. Of course, they needed hardware for the sluices, but that could be taken from the old gates and put on with little loss of time.

She hadn't gone but a few steps when the loud man said, "Says in the paper a crowd is already collecting for the trial. Wish I could get back there. Could be fun."

Maggie slowed, wondering if they were talking about Papa. Another man added, "I read that one of them had fights all up and down the Canal. Rough sort of fellow."

She wanted to tell that group her papa and Uncle Hen weren't rough at all. Shout it in their faces. That Papa could tell stories and sing songs in the old language and that he only had fights to help others, that Uncle Hen read books and loved the opera. That the charges were untrue . . .

No use making a scene, she decided, especially with people who probably wouldn't ever believe her. She stalked on down the towpath, furious, wondering what other lies the newspaper had printed and what other bits of nasty gossip folk were spreading.

By the time Maggie reached the *Betty*, she had built up a mighty head of steam. And there, coming from the opposite direction, was Billy Black, his steps labored, but his eyes as bright as ever and fixed on Momma, who was sitting on the stern rail.

"Good day ta ya again, Mrs. Haggrety," Billy Black said. "I'm wonderin' if I might be of some assistance ta ya now, ma'am."

If her momma was startled, she certainly didn't show it. She just looked the man straight in the eye and said, "I don't see there's much you can do."

"Tha Lord is a powerful presence." He glanced in Maggie's direction and nodded politely, then turned back to Momma. "And he's called on me ta help ya no matter what tha difficulty. With yer permission, of course."

"We don't give you permission," Maggie said sharply.

"Maggie . . ."

"Well, he can't fix the locks, so what's the point." She glared at Billy Black.

"Is *he* the one that's been bothering us?" Eamon

asked. He'd been sitting on the roof of the cabin, eating a piece of bread and petting Marcus.

Billy Black looked hurt by the comment, but Maggie was glad Eamon had said it.

"That wasn't ever my intention," he said. "Was trying ta do tha Lord's work, is all, though He never gives proper directions on how exactly ta do that. I am sorry, ma'am, if I've been a bother."

"Doesn't matter much now, does it?" said Momma. "As you see, we're stuck here along with everyone else."

"If there's nothing much ta do then there's nothing much ta lose if I try ta help, now is there?" He had regained some of his spirit and was able to smile. "If I fail ya . . ."

"Mr. Black," Momma interrupted him. "I need to go below and think through some things just now." Billy Black was about to add something else, but Momma cut him short. "Good day, Mr. Black," was all she said before disappearing below.

"I am sorry, miss," he said to Maggie. "Especially if I've bothered ya. I meant only ta help. A chance ta sarve yer family and tha Lord was all I wanted."

"We don't need you worrying about us," she said firmly. "Why can't you understand that!"

There, she'd told him flat out. It should have felt good to say what was on her mind and be done with him, only it didn't. The sad, empty look on Billy Black's face made her feel she should have been more careful with her words. Like she'd been trying to be with Eamon.

"I do, miss. I do understand." His quick patter was gone, and the man standing before her seemed tired and vulnerable. "Was jest going ta say that there's nothing ta lose really if I try ta help and fail."

"I know," Maggie said.

"And that if I fail ta speed yer journey along, miss, I'll walk down tha Canal and ya'll never see me again. Ever. I swear with tha Lord as my witness."

Maggie gulped and stared at the man. He was bound to fail, so to agree to his bargain would certainly make him disappear forever. The word "yes" suddenly seemed loaded with responsibility.

She thought about the horse and the way Billy Black had brought it back to life. What if he really did have powers she didn't understand? How would she feel if she didn't let him try to help them?

Finally, Maggie said, "I guess that's alright."

"Thank ya, miss. I am grateful ta ya. A chance ta sarve yer family and tha Lord is all I ask." He put on his hat and jacket, straightened his collar, and limped past Maggie toward the Lockport locks.

"He's pixilated and as loony as a drunk frog," Eamon commented.

A day ago, Maggie would have agreed and tossed in her own opinion. Today she wasn't so sure. "He's a persistent one," Maggie finally said.

He was gone a very long time. So Maggie went to see who had pulled in behind them. Eight freighters, so far, plus one packet. She knew three of the captains and made sure to tell each about Papa. She was talking to Captain Terry of the *Lady Chance* when she remembered his boat was out of Buffalo.

"Captain Terry," she said, her cheeks reddening slightly. "Do you know anything about the *Quick City*? She's out of Buffalo, too."

Captain Terry grimaced. "I know all I need to know about that bunch."

"Well, if it makes you feel better," she said quickly, "Momma punched the captain square in the nose at Port Byron. He was trying to bully his way ahead."

Captain Terry laughed loudly. "Can't think of anyone who deserves a good punch more. Be sure to thank your momma for me."

"I will, Captain Terry." Maggie paused. "I wondered,

though, if you knew anything about the *Quick City* crew. Especially a tallish one" — she held her hand a little over her head to indicate his height — "and on the young side."

Captain Terry shook his head slowly. "Let me think. . . ."

"His name's Michael. Least that's what I was told." She wanted to mention he had an amazing smile that could light up the night, but there was no way she could ever say anything that embarrassing. "He might have light-colored hair."

Captain Terry shook his head again, but stopped as he puzzled over the name. "Michael," he murmured. "Might be the boy come asking me for a job in March. Seemed nice enough, but I already had my crew. Michael Connelly was his name, if I recall correct. Is that who you mean?"

Maggie managed a smile. "I think so," she said, hoping he couldn't hear her heart pounding.

She was back at the *Betty* a few minutes later. Now she knew his full name and that someone she trusted thought he was nice, too. Her happiness at having solved this little mystery dissolved quickly when Eamon appeared at her side.

"There he is," Eamon grunted, pointing. "That Billy Black loon."

She looked up to find his squat, little figure coming

up the path toward them. "Eamon, you shouldn't say such things."

"You were the one said he was strange, not me! And he is."

Maggie watched as Billy Black stopped at a freighter and spoke to the captain, nodding his head and gesturing toward the *Betty* with the hand holding his hat. He finished talking to that captain and went to the next boat.

"I'm going downstream to see who's pulled in," Eamon announced.

Maggie didn't respond, she was so intent on watching Billy Black repeat his performance at one boat after another. When he was a few boats away, Maggie swallowed hard. Why on earth was the man smiling? she wondered. There was nothing he could have done to get the locks repaired faster or speed their journey along — nothing, that is, unless he'd somehow managed to work another miracle.

No One 16
Was That Good

"**M**omma," Maggie said, when Billy Black was two boats away. "That Billy Black is back."

When there was no answer, she poked her head inside the cabin door. "Momma, did you hear me?" There was still no response, so she called out louder, "Momma!"

Momma groaned and a moment later emerged from the cuddy, rubbing sleep from her eyes. "Must have fallen asleep," she said as she came up on deck. She seemed older to Maggie and her movements tentative. "Any word on what's happening?"

"They think it might reopen in two hours, if everything goes along smoothly. And that man" — she nodded toward Billy Black, who was still jawing with the captain of the freighter — "is a few boats ahead just now."

"He's still around?" Momma asked. "I thought I —"

"It's my fault," Maggie confessed. When Momma

stared at her, Maggie rushed to explain, "I didn't see any harm in his trying, so I said he could. He promised he'd leave us alone if he couldn't do anything —"

"And I keep my promises," Billy Black said from the towpath next to them. Maggie let out a tiny gasp, she was so startled. Billy Black continued, "Tha Lord's seen fit ta smile on us taday." He gestured to three men standing with him. "These captains and all tha others in front of ya have agreed ta let yer boat lock through ahead of 'm."

"And those that didn't agree," one captain with a neatly trimmed beard tossed in, "were persuaded it was the honorable thing to do." The other two men nodded in agreement.

Billy Black smiled. "We can move ya ta the front right now and be ready when tha locks open, ma'am. Tha lead boat above has agreed that ya should go ferst as well."

"Mr. Black," Momma began, her eyes blinking rapidly in confusion. "I'm not sure . . . I mean, this is very generous, but . . ."

Maggie knew the notion of cutting in front of everybody else was something Momma could never imagine doing, and that Papa got into fights with bullies about.

"Thought you might object, Mrs. Haggrety. That's why I brung along Captain Thomas, Captain Wills, and Captain Arnold." Each man tipped his cap and said hello as his name was mentioned. "Thay're a committee, if ya will, representing tha others in line." He nodded toward Captain Thomas.

"Mr. Black's right about that, Mrs. Haggarty. We know the situation and all of us want to help speed you through. It's the least we can do."

"Thank you, Captain Thomas." Momma seemed to be gathering in her thoughts and energy. "That's very kind of all of you. But I'm still not sure . . ." She gulped.

Maggie knew exactly what her momma was thinking. Here was the perfect answer to one of their problems, and yet it still did not sit well with her.

"You'll forgive me," Captain Thomas put in, "but your Tim has done us all a good turn or two. That time he lent me tackle for my mules when mine broke, for instance."

"Or when he helped me fix my rudder after it cracked on a rock," Captain Arnold added. "Took nearly two hours of his day."

"And Henry's done things for us, too," Captain Wills pointed out. "And so have you, Mrs. Haggarty. You brought potato soup when my driver was sick, remember?"

"What tha good captains might be saying," Billy Black said, "is that ya've earned tha right ta some consideration."

Momma lowered her eyes, that independent spirit — the one that had allowed her to punch Papa so long ago, that made her sew perfect stitches and have the *Betty* always gleaming — was bending and resisting at the same time. To accept their help might not feel right, but how else would they make Buffalo in time for the bonus?

"As much as I appreciate this . . ." Momma began more firmly.

Maggie felt her spirits sagging as the one chance to save the boat was about to slip away. She glanced up and found Billy Black looking directly at her. His eyes widened slightly when he knew he had her attention, then they slid to Momma and back to Maggie again.

He wants me to do something, she realized. She had a flash of annoyance at the man's nerve, but then remembered that she was the one who had set Billy Black on his quest in the first place. And while he still made her uneasy, she had to admit that so far he had been true to his word.

"Momma," Maggie whispered, tugging her mother's sleeve. "We should say yes."

"What did you say?" Momma asked.

"We should accept the offer," Maggie said in a louder voice. "There's no other way to make Buffalo on time. We should do it for Papa and Uncle Hen. Because this is an emergency."

"Yes, absolutely," Captain Thomas agreed. "A once-in-a-lifetime emergency." He took a small step forward. "With your permission, ma'am, we'll move you forward."

Momma hesitated a moment and took a deep breath, as a pained expression crossed her face. When Momma finally exhaled, she seemed even more exhausted than before. "I guess you're right, Maggie. This is no time to be stubborn. Not with so much at stake. We accept, Mr. Black."

Captain Thomas scrambled aboard, grabbing a pole, while the other two captains hitched up James and Issachar for the pull to the bottom of the locks. "Billy, will you cast off those lines?" Captain Thomas asked.

"I will, Captain." Billy untied the line to the tree, and Maggie hauled it in. When the front line was undone, the boat's nose was pushed out from the bank. As if from nowhere, Eamon came running up and leaped for the boat, just barely catching hold.

"Where're we going?" Eamon wanted to know as he hauled himself onto the deck. Captain Thomas answered cheerfully, "To the front of the line, son. To the very front."

"Really!?" Eamon said, amazed. "Did that Billy Black put everybody under a spell or something?"

There was no way Billy Black could leap on board. Not with his bum leg. The boat slowly drifted upstream and away from him, Billy Black getting smaller and lonelier-looking with each boat they passed.

Maggie had to admit feeling a little bad as she watched Billy Black limping along the towpath. He'd worked a miracle for them, plain and simple, so the least they could do was give him a ride. And maybe dinner. But still, the idea of having Billy Black in the boat's cabin made her shiver. He'd helped them, it was true, but that didn't mean she trusted him.

They had advanced past a dozen boats when a crew member on board a bright yellow packet called out, "Good luck to ya, Mrs. Haggarty."

The captain of the next boat took off his cap and said, "Don't you worry none. You'll be to the top soon enough."

As the *Betty* glided forward, other captains and crew members looked up from what they were doing to nod, wave, or shout encouragement. "We'll be praying for you, Anna. Don't you give up!" shouted a woman who'd poked her head out from her cabin.

At first it was awkward to have so many people knowing about her papa and the bonus, but then Maggie felt a surge of pride as more and more good wishes were delivered. So many people knew her papa and Hen were decent, honest men and wanted them back on the Canal. How could she have ever doubted Papa and Hen? These folk certainly didn't.

An image of the fight came to her, of that terrible moment when she'd doubted Papa. He was dripping sweat, mouth open gulping in air, and his eyes . . . That was the very moment Long-fingered John stepped between her and Papa and landed the punch that knocked him to the ground.

She tried to ignore that disturbing image to concentrate on that last second he'd been standing. What was it about his eyes, she wondered, that made her recall them?

The skin around the right eye was swollen from the pounding it had taken, that she remembered clearly. And then she saw it, in the tiny blink of time before Long-fingered John moved to block her view of him. Papa had looked at her. She was certain of it. He had taken his eyes off his opponent to look directly at her.

There was something unsettling about that look Papa had given her. But exactly what it was puzzled and confused her. Was he trying to tell her something?

She was instantly back in Lockport when a driver shouted, "Don't you take any guff from those lawyers in New Boston, Mrs. Haggarty." Maggie blinked and saw the man waving his hat and grinning.

Momma acknowledged the well-wishers with brief waves and softly murmured thank-yous. She could deliver a strongly worded lecture on Sheriff Einhornn, but now that she was accepting a kindness from these people, she was ill at ease, shy.

"You can go below, Momma, if you want," Maggie suggested. "Eamon and I'll take care of things up here."

"I'd appreciate that," Momma said and then made her way to the cabin.

Eamon stayed in the stern with Captain Wills at the sweep, while Maggie went forward to stand near the stable door. This was the first time in days that she wasn't doing something to keep the boat moving, that she had a chance to lean back and watch the world floating by.

There was something comforting in the way those in line were showing their support for her papa and Hen, but she wasn't silly enough to think their problems were over, not by a long shot. There were still more than thirty miles before they reached Buffalo, more than enough time for something else to go wrong.

And there was Billy Black.

She glanced down along the towpath until she spotted him, bent over, red-faced, and limping along behind them. Like a big rock rolling downhill. He'd seemed so genuinely pleased when they'd accepted the invitation to move forward, but he had to want something more than just to help them. No one was that good.

The Long Night 17

The long shadows of night had engulfed Lockport by the time the *Betty* was poled into the bottom lock and the gate closed behind her. A great cheer went up as the water level slowly rose and the boat came even with the top of the lock. Another cheer accompanied the flooding of the second lock.

Maggie led James and Issachar up the steep path to wait at the top for the *Betty*. The triumphant clanking of the metal sluice levers and the gurgle of water filling the great rectangular spaces confirmed that they were on their way. But her excitement was tempered by the voice in the dark behind her.

"Beggin' yer parden, miss."

Maggie jumped when she noticed Billy Black hovering next to the lockkeeper's shack.

"I am sorry, miss. Didn't intend ta startle ya none."

"You didn't," Maggie lied. "Honest." He had the

strangest ability to appear out of nowhere. "I thought you might be here," she said quietly.

Billy Black took a few tentative steps toward her. "I was hoping ta talk with ya some."

"With me? Why?"

"When tha Lord instructed me ta offer my sarvice ta ya, miss, He meant it to be fer as long as ya needed help. It's still thirty-one miles inta Buffalo, and if yer ta make it by mornin' you'll have ta travel mosta tha night. I reckon ya could use an extra driver, miss."

He was right. Not only did they have to travel thirty-one miles, they also had to unload the boat before noon tomorrow. There was every reason to accept Billy Black's offer, and yet she hesitated. Not even Maggie's wobbly legs let her get beyond her suspicions of the man.

"You need to ask my momma," Maggie said. "It's not for me to say."

Billy Black's smile appeared in the dimming light. "Absolutely, miss," was all he said in reply.

Their boat was maneuvered from the lock by the three captains. Once it had stopped, Momma came on deck to thank them, after which captains Thomas, Wills, and Arnold headed down the path to rejoin their own boats.

Maggie began hitching the team to the lines Eamon threw her as Billy Black stepped forward. She noticed

Eamon eyeing the man suspiciously and wondered if he might blurt out something else about him being a loon.

"Momma," Maggie said, "Mr. Black here wants to talk to you."

"Ah, Mr. Black," said Mama. "I want to thank you for getting us through Lockport so quickly. I, ah . . . we don't know what we would have done without you."

"Something would have gotten ya hare," he said. "I've no doubt about it, ma'am. But it's gettin' ta Buffalo that consurns me now. I'm thinkin' ya could use a driver to help get ya through tha night and I was hopin' ya'd let me help ya again."

Momma was quiet a few moments, most likely thinking about the long night ahead and realizing she had little real choice. "You've helped us enough, Mr. Black," she said at last. "We can't impose on you any more than we already have. It wouldn't be right."

"But Mrs. Haggrety, ma'am . . ."

"Mr. Black," she began, with a touch of annoyance. She stopped and sighed, then said in a weary and embarrassed voice, "Mr. Black, we've only a little money left and I might need that to get the cargo unloaded. I can't accept any more help without paying you. It's not what we do." Billy Black went to protest, but Momma held her hand up and added, "Tim — Mr. Haggarty — wouldn't want me to. So while we appreciate what you've done and what you're offering . . ."

Maggie did not trust the man's eagerness, and all of his talk of the Lord made her feel uneasy. And yet she couldn't see how they would get to Buffalo on time without him. "But Momma," Maggie suggested tentatively.

"Maggie." She gave Maggie a warning look.

"We could give him meals instead of pay, couldn't we? Papa wouldn't mind that. We can't get to Buffalo in time on our own."

Momma's look froze Maggie and made her feel momentarily as if she were the stranger in the conversation and not Billy Black.

Billy Black coughed. "I'm not against that as reward," he said. "Even Jesus had ta eat."

"And he'll probably follow us no matter what we say," Maggie added. She looked at Billy Black. "Right?"

"Well, ah . . ." Billy Black looked down at his feet.

There was another pause as Momma studied both Maggie and Billy Black. "I'm still not sure this is right," Momma finally said, "but Maggie has a point. We'll not make it ourselves. So I guess we should accept your help. But only until we get this situation . . . settled."

"Aye, ma'am. Only till it's settled and over."

Not fifteen minutes after the agreement was struck, the mules were moving the *Betty* west again. Eamon watched Billy Black carefully before going below to get something to eat. Billy Black did the driving out of Lockport, and even though it made her uneasy having a stranger driving, Maggie went to the stable to check on Tom.

"How's your hoof, boy?" she asked, as she removed it from the bucket and dried his leg and hoof. She laid the leg across her knee and examined the sole carefully.

"That looks fine," she murmured. Next she pressed with her thumb where the metal had been lodged. Tom's leg never twitched, so it didn't hurt him. Another good sign. "Once we're through the Deep Cut, you and Rudy will get to pull again."

The safest thing would have been to let Tom's foot rest another day, but Maggie knew they didn't have that luxury. Not if they hoped to unload before the noon deadline.

It was nearly midnight when the switch was made and Maggie trailed along behind to keep an eye on Tom. She'd told Billy Black about Tom's injury, sensing he would spot the slightest change in the mule's stride. Still she didn't want to leave Tom to someone he didn't know.

They had gone a while when Billy Black cleared his

throat. "Pardon me, miss, but that mule's leg seems strong ta me." There was something in his voice — a hesitation — that surprised Maggie. "What do ya think, miss?"

"He's walking fine, Mr. Black. I'll just tag along for a little longer, though, to be sure."

"Of course," Billy Black said.

After this was silence, except for the steady, soft clomp of hooves and the occasional sliding crunch of shoes on loose gravel. Maggie was the first to break the silence. "Did the Lord really talk to you about us, Mr. Black? I mean, really talk to you?"

It took Billy Black a few steps to respond. "That He did, miss. Was in a dream. Most folk think I'm daft, and I can't blame'm. I didn't believe it either tha first time He came ta me. But it's tha plain truth, I swear."

"What does He look like?"

"He? You mean tha Lord? Oh, I've never seen His face. Not yet anyways. It's jest a great white light that fills my head when He instructs me. But I've hope, miss. That one day I'll be forgiven and He'll appear ta me, though I don't know when that might happen."

Once when her papa had a particularly bad hangover, he'd described a pulsing light behind his eyes that accompanied his throbbing head. Maybe Billy Black hadn't completely reformed as he claimed; maybe his encounters with the Lord came after he'd had an encounter with a bottle. Maggie didn't suggest this to the man. Instead she asked, "How do you know it's the Lord, then? I mean, it could be anyone. Even the Devil. Those girls downstream talk to all sorts of dead spirits."

"Can't explain it," he said, shrugging his shoulders. "Jest a feeling I have. And I wouldn't carry out no sinful suggestions, if that worries ya, miss. Tha Lord led me from my sinful ways and I won't betray Him none."

When Momma called, Maggie dropped back to talk.

"No use you walking along too much," Momma told her. "We've a long night ahead. I'm full awake now, so you should go below and rest. I'll call you up in an hour or two. It's going to be tight into Buffalo."

Eamon was finishing up the last of the lamb stew when Maggie came below. He glanced up at her, then said, "What was that loon telling you?"

"Oh, Eamon, he's just a little . . . I don't know, odd, I guess. Wants to do us a good turn so he can get into heaven or something." She shrugged.

"Well, I'm going on deck to keep an eye on him."

"Why don't you check on James and Issachar while you're up there? Make sure they have water."

"Yeah." Eamon smiled and got up from the little table. "That way I can watch him from the stable." He left without scraping his dish into the slops bucket, but Maggie let him go. The mules would get looked after and that was more important.

She took some cheese and bread to the cuddy and nibbled at it while lying in the dark space. She had hoped to make some sort of sense of Billy Black, only her racing thoughts kept intruding. Too many miles separated them from Buffalo; too many things could still go wrong.

If only Michael were here to help them. He looked just a little older than Maggie, but she was sure he could help them get the boat to Buffalo on time. As she drifted off to sleep, however, she realized that Michael wasn't going to appear out of nowhere to save the day. That only happened in those stories Uncle Hen told about knights and ladies in distress. No, if they were going to make Buffalo, it would be up to her, Momma, and Eamon. And broken-down Mr. Black was the closest they'd get to a knight in shining armor.

It was her mother's voice that woke Maggie. Her eyes flew open and her body tensed. Something's wrong. What had Billy Black done?

"Maggie, we're going to change teams." There was no alarm to her momma's voice, no sense of urgency.

Maggie rolled from her bunk, stretched, and shook her head alert. Eamon was in his bunk sound asleep, his breathing deep. He would be out for hours, so Maggie tossed a blanket over him. Not so many years before, she would have been able to push aside her troubles and sleep away the night, too.

"Where are we?" Maggie asked when she got on deck.

"Just beyond Pendleton." Momma yawned. "After the change, you take the sweep a while. I need to rest these legs of mine."

"Sure, Momma. Take all the time you need." A cover of clouds blocked the moon so that when Maggie peered ahead, the Canal was one forbidding shadow on top of another, with only a few gray patches in between. "Dark as anything up ahead."

"Your eyes'll adjust," Momma said. "And Mr. Black is watching for trouble."

Billy Black had slowed Tom and Rudy and undid the line to the boat. He coiled the long piece of rope and tossed it on board, then continued walking with the mules. As the boat moved away from him, Momma asked, "How are they, Mr. Black? Any sign of trouble?"

"None, ma'am. The one with tha hurt foot is stepping down regular." Even in the dark, Maggie thought she saw him tip his hat politely. "I'll be along in a minute with these two." With that the boat drifted along and Billy Black faded into the darkness of the towpath.

Maggie took up a pole to maneuver the *Betty* as she slowed. She had wanted to ask her momma direct for several days now, only the nearness of other people and Momma's fierce sense of privacy always made her hesitate. Being alone with her now in the dark made Maggie feel bolder.

"Momma, is something wrong I should know about?"

"Wrong? You mean about Papa and Hen?"

"No, I mean with you. You were sick downstream and Eamon said you were sick the other morning, too. And you're tired most of the time lately."

"I'm not sick with a fever, if that's what you mean." There was a slight pause, and Maggie heard the boat scrape against some bushes growing close to the water. Her momma sighed. "It's just that this one's been so hard. You were easy and Eamon wasn't so bad. But this one . . ."

"This one?" Maggie asked, confused, and in that instant the answer came to her. "You mean a baby? You're having another baby?" Her voice had gone up an octave in surprise. But now she dropped it to a whisper. "Why didn't you tell us? Does Papa know?"

"I haven't told anybody. Except Jozie and now you. I felt so awful sick early on I wasn't sure I'd be able to carry it and when all this happened to your papa . . ." She shrugged her shoulders ever so slightly. "I didn't think it the best time to tell him."

A recollection of her momma leaping across the water to confront that bullying captain of the *Quick City* came to Maggie and made her gasp. "When you punched that man . . . you could have been hurt. . . ."

"Don't think I haven't thought about that a hundred times and scolded myself, too. I think I was just so crazy angry about everything. . . ." The bow of the boat touched the muck along the bank and came to a gentle stop. "Well, that won't happen again soon, believe me. Not a word about this to anyone. I'll tell Papa when the time's right."

When would that be? Maggie wondered. After the trial probably. But what if the trial didn't go the way they wanted? What if Papa had to stay in jail?

She went forward to the stable to help with the change. The right time might never come for telling about the baby, she realized. And the right time might never come for meeting Michael Connelly in person, or for living beyond the Canal.

The switch was made, Tom and Rudy were stabled, and the journey continued, this time through a brooding forest. Well, Maggie told herself, there's going to be a baby on board, right time or not.

She steered the boat around a sharp curve where overhanging tree branches brushed along the cabin roof. She felt annoyed with herself when she realized she hadn't asked her momma when the baby would be born. Or whether she wanted a boy or girl. Or even if she'd thought of any names.

Michael would be a good name for a boy, she decided, smiling at the idea and at the recollection of *her* Michael. Michael Haggarty had a strong feel to it.

She could picture the baby crawling up the cabin stairs and along the stern deck; she could hear it crying to be nursed. There would be cloth diapers and pins, baby clothes and a crib to sleep in. Uncle Hen could make the crib. . . .

"Oh, my," she said. There was no telling when he would be able to make a crib.

Don't you worry none, little baby. No matter what happens, we'll be here to take care of you. Momma, Eamon, and me. Don't you worry none.

Billy Black, 18
Where Are You?

They traveled throughout the night with Momma, Maggie, and Billy Black changing jobs from time to time. When it was Billy Black's turn to rest or eat he did so in the stable. Near five in the morning, Eamon wobbled on deck and started in complaining.

"You shoulda got me up!" he said. "I wanted ta drive all night."

"You weren't the only one to rest, Eamon," Momma said as patiently as she could.

"No one rested as long as I did."

"We rested according to our needs. Now stop making noise and help Maggie get those mules ready for the change. We've no time to waste." Maggie could tell Momma was already worrying about the trick of unloading. And for good reason.

The air was heavy with mist, and a gloomy, gray light began to soften the edges of darkness when they passed a squat log cabin sitting on a hill. Years ago, it had been a bunkhouse for canal workers, but it was now occupied by a married couple, their three children, and two goats. The cabin was only a few bends from Black Rock and from there it was five miles to Buffalo.

"You shoulda got me up sooner," Eamon mumbled the moment they were in the stable.

"I couldn't leave off steering. Besides, you were snoring to rattle the windows."

She thought he might crack a smile, or at least blurt out something rude to distract himself, but his lips remained firmly pressed together. "I wanted to be up and helping Papa."

"Well, you're up and helping now. And stop bothering Momma. She's" — going to have a baby, she almost said —"not feeling so good."

Maggie put a harness on Rudy and was happy to see the mule wasn't as jittery as he'd been a few days before. Only after pulling the strap tight did she notice Eamon still standing with Tom's harness in his hands, staring off. "What's the matter with you?" she asked.

He glanced quickly at her, then set about his chore. Something's wrong, Maggie realized. "You okay?" she asked.

When he made no immediate reply, Maggie tried

another tack. "It was nothing but black out there and I just lost track of the time. I didn't *not* wake you up on purpose."

"It's just that I had a dream," Eamon said. "About Papa, I think."

Maggie took anything that came to mind unasked seriously, whether it was a dream or one of her flashing recollections. It wasn't that they predicted the future, though she did think they had a purpose of some kind. "What happened?"

"Can't remember exactly," he answered. "Something bad, though. 'Cause when I woke up I felt sad."

It was another one of those odd moments when Maggie sensed she should do something to throw off his upset. But what? Papa would have shaken him in a friendly way and said something like, "Come on, cheer up. The day's too short to waste in a bad mood." Momma would have told him such thoughts were nonsense and given him a chore to keep his mind busy. Maggie wasn't comfortable with either approach.

"He's going to be fine," she said.

"How do you know?"

"I just do." She looked right into his eyes, holding her stare as firmly as Momma might. "He's going to be fine, but first we need to collect that bonus, then we need to get downstream to him. Let's get that gear on Tom so I can check his hoof again."

After the change, the flat fields gave way to buildings. Despite having made the journey scores of times in the past, Maggie found her heart racing as they entered Buffalo. Not even the gray, thin rain that began falling could dampen her happiness when the Tucker & Wyndham Warehouse came into view.

"We made it," Momma said to Billy Black, "and not yet nine o'clock."

"Tha Lord and these mules sped us along, Mrs. Haggrety."

Maggie was glad he gave the mules some of the credit.

The boat was stopped near the wide, rear door to the warehouse, and Eamon took all four mules up a side street to Kelly's Livery.

The manager of Tucker & Wyndham appeared beside the *Betty*, his hat casting a menacing shadow across his face. "I was hoping to see you yesterday," Mr. Eisler said impatiently. His long, thin face was ashen and lined, the product of twenty-three years of scribbling numbers in a tiny upstairs office. "A wagon train left this morning and with it several sales."

"We're here today as promised, Mr. Eisler," Momma

said with a bit of ice to her words, "and you can thank your lucky stars and a lot of kind folks for that."

Mr. Eisler wasn't one for chitchat. Instead, he glanced around in a concerned, twitchy way. "Is Mr. Haggarty about, ma'am?"

"Not this run, Mr. Eisler. His brother Henry is absent as well." There was absolutely no way that news about the arrest of Tim and Henry Haggarty hadn't reached Buffalo, but Maggie assumed Mr. Eisler was too busy scratching away in his account books to take note of Canal gossip. "Don't worry. We'll get the shipment in and I'll bring the papers to you after."

"That's good to hear, Mrs. Haggarty," the man said, looking doubtful that a woman, a girl, a young boy, and an old man could do the job. "There are several customers inside now asking after plows. Could you bring those in first?" He gave instructions on where the plows and stoves were to be stored before going back inside.

No mention of the noon deadline for unloading was ever made, though this didn't surprise Maggie. Both parties knew the terms of the agreement. Momma also knew better than to ask if some of Mr. Eisler's workers could be spared to help them unload. There would be no bonus if his men had to lift a finger.

"Alright," Momma told Maggie, "let's roll back the tarp and get started. It'll be heavy and slippery with this rainwater on it."

"But, Momma, you can't carry anything heavy!"

"Maggie, we have too much to do. . . ."

"You can't and you know it." Maggie leaned a little closer to her momma. "What would Papa say if" — Maggie looked in the direction of her momma's belly — "if anything happened."

There was no mistaking the guilty look that flashed across Momma's face, nor the way her lips pursed when she realized her daughter was right.

"And you said we might use the money we have to get help unloading."

"But we might need that to help your father. . . ."

"Momma, stop and be sensible!" Maggie blinked several times, astonished and a little frightened that she'd raised her voice to Momma. "What I meant was . . ."

"No, no, there's no need, Maggie," Momma said. "You're right. We'll need help." She looked past Maggie. "Mr. Black . . ." Her head swung one way and another as she searched the towpath. "Now where has he gone to?"

He had vanished. There beside the boat one moment, gone the next. "Mr. Black!" Maggie called. "Billy Black, where are you?" Several men from boats and buildings nearby looked up, but none of them was Billy Black.

"We've no time to waste on him," Momma said impatiently. "See that boat up there? Ask if any of those men can help us. We'll pay a dollar per man. I'll go this way."

The girl asked at the boat, but the captain said they had a bonus to make, too, so he couldn't spare a man. "Just as soon as we're finished, we'll come down, though. We heard what happened ta yer pa, so we'd be happy ta help ya then."

Maggie thanked him and went to the next boat. And the next and the next. Everyone along this stretch of the Canal was unloading and couldn't spare a hand. The few layabouts she came across were too hungover to be of much use and certainly not worth a good dollar's pay.

When she returned to the *Betty*, Momma and Eamon were waiting there. They both looked cold and frail with rainwater dripping from their jackets. It didn't help Maggie's spirits that a thin, sallow-faced man with puffy eyes was with them.

"Everybody's busy just now," she told her mother. "They'll be along when they've unloaded, but it'll be a few hours at least."

"Same this way," Momma said. "This is Mickey Duff. He's agreed to help us some."

The man nodded. "From Syracuse, miss, by way of County Kerry."

And several dozen taverns in between, Maggie speculated, though all she said was, "Hello, Mr. Duff."

The tarp to the cargo bay was removed, and Maggie stared at the piled-up iron stoves and plows. One hundred and twenty-five stoves and eighty-five plows made a powerful heap of tangled metal. She didn't even have to add up numbers to know it would be more than two hundred back-and-forth trips and not more than three hours before the deadline. How were they going to manage it?

She grabbed the handle of a plow and began wrestling it loose from its companions.

"I'll help ya there, miss," Mickey Duff said, stepping up onto a plow. Instantly he slipped on the wet blade so that both his legs disappeared from sight. "No problem," he said quickly, looking embarrassed. He pulled his legs free and took hold of the front of the plow. "Maybe the young man there can help you with your end."

"And maybe it'll take us an hour to move one of these things," Maggie barked. There's no time for angry words, Maggie told herself. "Help lift it clear of the others," Maggie told Eamon when he'd joined her on the narrow deck. "Then jump to the towpath while I back down the plank."

"It'll be slippery," Momma cautioned, meaning the plank.

Both Maggie and Eamon strained to heft the plow up, while Mickey Duff grunted and muttered nervously, "Slow now, slow. No need to rush. No need."

Maggie put her left foot on the wood plank and stead-ied the plow as Eamon released his grip and jumped to the towpath. Her boot slipped some, just a bit really, but enough that she jerked her arm to balance the awk-ward weight. "Steady, miss," Mickey Duff said quickly. "Steady now."

Her boot gripped solidly so her next step went more easily. Mickey Duff began easing himself from the pile of plows, but when he wobbled, Momma moved forward to help them. "We've got it, Momma," Maggie said. That was when Mickey Duff slipped, then lurched forward, and Maggie felt her boot begin sliding down the slippery plank. Slowly at first, and then more quickly.

"Eamon!" she squeaked in a shaky voice as she picked up speed.

"Steady, steady." Mickey Duff's words had an edge of terror to them as he envisioned himself being pulled headfirst off the boat.

"Maggie!" Momma shouted. She stood back as the plow suddenly shot past her. "Catch her, Eamon!"

It all happened in a flash — the sliding, the exchange of words, the sudden, desperate feeling that she would land on the towpath and the plow, and Mickey Duff would come crashing down to crush her.

"Let me help ya there," a gruff voice said in Maggie's ear at the same moment the weight of the plow was lifted from her hands. She continued smoothly down the slick plank and stumbled backward when her heels hit the towpath, though Eamon was quick enough to stop her from landing in the mud.

Maggie's first thought was that Michael had appeared to rescue her, but then she saw who had saved her.

"Mr. Black!" she said, surprised.

"Yes, miss," Billy Black replied, huffing under the plow's weight. Another man was on the other side of the plank helping Billy Black bring the plow to the towpath and set it down. "I'm sorry ta take so long," he said to Maggie's mother. "I've been rounding up some help."

Besides Billy Black, there were five men lined up facing Momma. The Canal was inhabited by all sorts of unusual folk, but even Maggie thought these five were some of the scruffier characters she'd ever seen.

"These are acquaintances of mine. From my previous life, ma'am. Rough 'round tha edges, I admit, but good men and ready ta work for three dollars a man."

Momma studied each man top to bottom with a scowl, and Maggie worried that she would send them all away. "One dollar is all I'll pay," Momma said firmly.

"One dollar ta unload is fair enough," Billy Black said, "but they've agreed ta crew till ya get down ta New Boston, ma'am. That accounts for t'other two dollars."

"I don't know, Mr. Black." Maggie could tell her momma was trying to calculate whether the amount was fair, or even if a crew was necessary. They had to cover more than two hundred miles to get to New Boston.

"Beggin' yer pardon, ma'am." Billy Black rummaged in the pocket of his jacket and came up with a folded newspaper. "Says here tha trial's ta start on Thursday. That's three days from now." He handed the paper to Momma. Even a dunderhead would understand it, but Billy Black added, "Thar's no time ta lose, I'm afraid."

"I'll go to New Boston, too," Mickey Duff blurted out, "for another two dollars."

Momma looked at the newspaper article, and her face blanched as a shooting pain went through her body.

"You're right, Mr. Black," she said. "There's no time to waste. A dollar to unload and two to get us to New Boston." Her eyes slid to Mickey Duff. "If you can find a use for him, then he can stay as well. Now I think there's some serious work to get to, don't you?"

"Yes, ma'am," Billy Black said as he pulled his hat tight to his head. "Alright, lads, lets get ta this bafore tha clouds open up."

Smothered by the Wet and Dark 19

Despite a steady rain, the boat was unloaded at an astonishing pace, with two men at a time carrying an item. In a matter of minutes, a parade of plows and stoves went floating from the boat to the warehouse.

Eamon was still at the livery, while Momma had gone below to rest. "That Mr. Eisler and this rain has got to me," she'd said as she put her hand to her belly. "I need to be below to settle this one down."

Maggie stayed on deck, her canvas jacket buttoned tight, her hat pulled low. Mr. Black had been true to his word, and yet the girl still felt someone from the family needed to watch the unloading.

The men finished up at half past eleven and Mr. Eisler appeared at the side of the boat. He took out his pocket watch and checked the time. "It seems you made it with time to spare," he said drily. "You were very lucky to find these men."

Maggie bit back the urge to say something dis-respectful to the man, but only by a little. Instead, she said, "Yes, we know, Mr. Eisler."

Mr. Eisler produced a roll of cash and very carefully began counting out the hauling fee and bonus. "We might have sold four plows if you'd been here yesterday," he added as he held out the money to her. Maggie wanted to snatch it from his hands, she was so impatient.

Thankfully, another boat pulled in behind the *Betty* just then, so Mr. Eisler went off to pester its captain.

"Never mind him, miss," Billy Black said. "Can't think outside his books, is all." He looked to the men who had gathered behind him at the foot of the boarding plank. "I was wonderin', miss, if tha men might be paid their first dollar. They're eager ta find some . . . um, refreshments."

"We need to be heading downstream. This rain'll cause all kinds of delays."

"Yes, miss. But those mules need ta rest and so do these men. We probably shouldn't leave much b'fore four o'clock. Fer tha mules' sake."

Maggie wasn't sure it was the mules' care that was most on their minds, but she knew they were due the first part of their money. She counted out six dollars and handed it to Billy Black. "But we leave at *two* o'clock. No later. I expect every man to be here or we go without him. Understood?"

"Aye, I do. Rest assured, we'll be back. I'll be looking after the men myself."

"See that you do," she said firmly. He made no response, though Maggie felt immediately bad for the hard way she'd spoken. First she'd snapped at Momma, and now at Billy Black. What had gotten into her? It came to her then that many adults, even her papa and momma, used that same tone when they wanted it clear they meant business.

Before going off, the men poled the boat up so it wasn't blocking any of the warehouse's space and replaced the tarp to keep rain from collecting in the hold. They'd done everything efficiently, but Maggie circled the boat anyway to make sure all flaps were secured snuggly. Next she went to the stable to see that it was tidy. A few of Uncle Hen's books were out of place, and she assumed Billy Black had looked at them during the night. Otherwise the space was neat.

When she went to the cabin, she found Momma asleep in the cuddy, with Marcus lounging in Eamon's bunk. Maggie let the curtain fall back closed and sat at the little table to wait. Over the past few days, she'd found these moments of stillness the hardest to endure. Memories of Papa and Hen would come to her, one after another, which set her remembering and worrying.

She had that faint, familiar feeling of wanting to escape — to some chore that needed doing, to an argument with Eamon. Instead she made herself a cup of tea, leaned back in the chair, and listened to the rain patter against the windows.

Why wasn't she happier? she wondered. They'd raced to reach Buffalo on time, had gotten the bonus, which meant the boat payment would be made. Yet Maggie felt . . . What? She wasn't exactly sure how she felt. Empty was one way to describe it. And tired. Tired in the way she felt after hours of driving, knowing there were still many miles to go.

And frightened. They still had to get to New Boston in time for the trial. Even then they might not be done. Not if Papa and Hen were found guilty. And there was that new life growing in Momma, and her not feeling well.

She looked out the window to see if Eamon might be coming with the mules and was impatient when he wasn't. She checked the sleeping cuddy again. Momma was still curled up, a blanket pulled over her protectively.

Maggie went back to the table. Sitting alone, she felt responsible for everything suddenly — for getting Billy

Black and his friends back and working in time, for traveling downstream as fast as possible, for watching over Momma and the baby, for solving any problems that might come along.

She sipped her tea, trying to enjoy the way the liquid warmed the inside of her mouth. They had already dealt with and overcome so many obstacles, and yet they were far from finished. She needed to summon up some reserve of energy if they were going to make the run to New Boston in time.

No wonder Momma chose to retreat to the sleeping cuddy. No wonder Papa sipped his hard cider and Hen spent hours in his books. To be rid of the burden of day-to-day life, of being a responsible grown-up. She wondered if her parents and Hen would have felt differently if they lived on a farm or in one of the towns along the Canal.

A sudden thump of boots on deck startled her and she stood, anxious.

"Miss Haggrety," Billy Black called tentatively from the deck. More footsteps could be heard moving on the boat. "Miss? Are ya about?"

"I'll be right up," she replied in a whisper. She hurried to put on her jacket and hat and went up to the crew.

"The boys here wanted ta get movin' south, miss.

Dick thar" — he pointed to a short man with long hair hanging from his cap — "is good with numbers and he says we're on a tight run ta New Boston even if tha locks're clear all tha way down. Wouldn't want to miss the start of tha . . . well, we wouldn't want ta be delayed unnecessarily, now would we, miss?"

"No, we wouldn't," Maggie said. He'd been as good as his word and done precisely what he'd promised to do, and yet she still found herself wary of his suggestion. Why was that? she wondered. Was it her worry over Papa and Hen that was making her distrust anybody but family? "Eamon took the mules to Kelly's. Momma's resting, so we need to get moving as quietly as possible."

"Aye, miss. We will."

Eamon and the mules were fetched back a few minutes later. With some banging about and a few shouted exchanges, the men poled the boat around to face downstream and had James and Issachar hitched to the towline. Then the *Betty* was set in motion once again.

One of the men — the one called Dick — was at the sweep.

"He once owned his own boat," Billy Black explained when he saw Maggie studying the man. "Was a good captain till tha drink got him. But he's fine now," he added quickly. "Had just one. I watched him."

Still, it didn't feel right to Maggie. She wanted Papa and Uncle Hen on board instead of these strangers. "He seems able," she replied carefully. "We should keep an eye on him, though."

"I will, miss."

"I will, too, Mr. Black." There was that twinge again over talking to an adult so directly. "Momma wouldn't approve."

"Aye, miss. Yer momma doesn't need anything else ta trouble her. If ya see anything that bothers ya, just tell me and I'll set it right."

"I will."

And so they traveled throughout the day, into the late afternoon and through the wet night, stopping every two hours to change the mules. They were going with the current, and the boat was empty and light, so they made good time. In addition to Dick at the sweep, two other men were always on deck poling the boat for extra speed.

Maggie was there, too, as was Mr. Black, and later, Momma. They reached Lockport just as a church bell rang once. It made a frail, lonely sound that was smothered by the wet and dark. Maggie calculated the miles they still had to cover.

"Will we make it in time, Mr. Black?" Momma asked. She'd been thinking about the miles ahead, too.

"With tha Lord's help, Mrs. Haggrety. And some

luck." There was a curious flat quality to his words, as if he didn't really believe them himself.

Luck, though, was indeed with them at Lockport. No one was trying to come up the one open lock, so they entered it and began descending the watery steps immediately.

Momma took the sweep during the locking through, while Maggie and Billy Black poled. Since the lock-keeper was off duty, the rest of the crew swarmed over the timbers and stonework like shadowy ants, two to a lock.

"You might consider getting some rest now, miss," Billy Black said to Maggie as they poled the boat from the bottom lock. "And yer mother, too. We'll only need two men fer mosta tha night. No need ta be on deck."

"Who'll watch the men?" Maggie asked. Someone had to be alert for any danger to the boat and mules and the bonus money.

"Dick can be trusted while he's at the sweep. When we change crews, I'll come on deck." She didn't reply in any way. "We have ta trust tha Lord that things will go right."

For some reason, Billy Black's trust in the Lord did not provide Maggie with much comfort.

"Eamon," Maggie called, looking past Billy Black to where her brother was on the towpath. "You should get some sleep while you can."

"I want to stay out longer. I'm not tired anyways." Eamon was riding the trailing mule, and Maggie could see he was ready to argue his case some more.

"If that's what you want."

"I'll stay here with Dick if it'll put yer mind at ease," Billy Black added.

Maggie didn't know why she was being so untrusting. He couldn't very well steal the boat; everybody on the Canal knew Papa's boat on sight.

"Okay, then, I'll go below. Dick can take care of things here, so you should rest, too."

"Thank you, miss. I was hopin' you'd see it that way." He spoke to Dick about when he'd relieve him, then turned toward the stable, only to stop a few steps along. "Last night He came ta me again, miss. Tha Lord. He didn't leave me any instructions. Was just that white light filling up my head."

Maggie found herself suddenly interested in hearing that Billy Black had had another visit. "What did He want?" she asked cautiously.

"Can't say fer certain." Billy Black shrugged. "Woke up feeling better than I have in a long time, so I suppose it wasn't anything bad."

Maggie felt her spirits rising.

"Course, ya can never tell with tha Lord. He works in funny ways sometimes."

Maggie went below, wondering why Billy Black had to add that last bit of uncertainty. Why couldn't he just end with his feeling good? It was especially unfair to suggest that the Lord might be playing games, since there was little chance of winning against that kind of opponent.

Despite trusting Billy Black's judgment about Dick, she still retrieved the money tin from its hiding place and took it into the cuddy. After climbing into her bunk, she placed the tin under the covers next to her. She was so tired, her body seemed to melt into the thin mattress though sleep didn't settle on her immediately. Whenever she closed her eyes, troubling images buzzed in and out of her mind. The judge's gavel crashing down as he said the word "guilty," the shocked look on Papa's face, Long-fingered John's smug smile. . . .

Another worry wormed its way into her head. Will Momma and the baby be okay? Momma had seemed even more distracted than usual today.

Back and forth she tossed, searching for a comfortable position as the money tin jabbed at her side. Eamon came in dripping wet, but still managed to be asleep in a matter of seconds. It isn't fair that I have to worry about all of this, she thought, missing Papa more than ever.

She drifted off into a fitful sleep, then woke briefly at the sound of Billy Black taking over for Dick. Where were they? she wondered groggily. She felt for the money tin, and when she couldn't locate it, she sat up abruptly. A few seconds later, she found it safely pressed against the wall. She woke again at dawn, tired and anxious. The one good thing, Maggie noticed, was that the rain had stopped and a hazy sun was poking through the thinning clouds.

If Billy Black was tired, he never showed it. He was either at the sweep or else on deck making sure the men did their tasks correctly. Both teams of mules were played out by early afternoon. Billy Black kept the *Betty* moving by borrowing mules from friends in various towns with a promise to send them back upstream by other boats.

Yet as the hours and miles sailed past, as they went through one and another town or solved small problem after problem, Maggie found herself worrying more and more. There was no control, she had come to realize. Not over Papa's fate or over anything much besides keeping the boat moving in the right direction. And even that wasn't guaranteed.

On the third morning, she was on deck with Billy Black at the sweep when they sailed past the Chittenango Feeder. That meant they were two miles from New Boston.

"We've been lucky," Billy Black said. He was wearing his jacket even though the day was warm, and sweat beaded on his forehead. "No heavy traffic ta slow us, and fair weather. Won't be long now ta yer father and uncle."

It was then that Maggie realized Billy Black had done precisely as promised. He'd gotten them to Buffalo in time to get the bonus, and then back to Papa. Where would they be now if their lives hadn't intersected with his? She wished she could give him a proper reward for all of his hard work, but the best she could manage was a weak "Thank you, Mr. Black, for helping us."

"I'm jest thankful ya let this sinner be of some use, miss."

Maggie felt herself blush. After a while, she said, "Mr. Black. Have you . . . um, have you heard from the Lord again? About Papa and Uncle Hen?"

He glanced uneasily at Maggie. "No, miss, I haven't." His voice sounded a little sad. "All we can do now is hope fer tha best and trust in tha good Lord ta make it happen."

She almost wished she hadn't asked him, but at least he hadn't foreseen a bad outcome.

In a little while, they came upon the beginning of a line of boats. The first was a blue-and-red freighter, the *Raven*, out of Troy. A yellow coal barge was just in front of the *Raven*, with a packet next and then another freighter. They inched around a bend and found a long line of boats tied up on both sides of the Canal, with barely enough room up the middle for the *Betty* to squeeze by. Freighters and packets, work boats, and floating bakeries. One sort of colorful boat after another stretching up the Canal.

"Mr. Black," Momma called from the towpath. "Maybe two of your men could haul our line over these boats."

"Yes, ma'am." He immediately relayed the order and two men went into action.

"The boats are all empty," Maggie said. "No one about except for mules and horses."

She was right. Seventy or eighty boats on each side of the Canal, but not one person on board or even on the towpath. No one watching the shipments. No one polishing the lamps. No one killing time. Just empty boats.

"It's very strange, miss. Very strange indeed."

Not just strange, Maggie thought. It's so still and quiet that it's spooky. When buildings came into view, she saw immediately there were no people lingering about there, either. This place is more than spooky, she thought. It's dead.

"Oh, my," Maggie muttered and clamped her mouth shut. They're all at the trial. Like those dandies at Lockport, they'd all gone to watch the show.

20 *A Grim Picture*

There was no space for their boat, so Momma ordered the *Betty* to stop at Froude's General Store right beside another freighter. A small sign in the window of the store said CLOSED.

"Mr. Black," Momma said. "Could you find a proper place for the boat up ahead, while I go with the children to find their father?"

"Aye, ma'am," he replied.

A few days earlier, Maggie might have bristled at the notion of leaving the boat with Billy Black and these men, but all she was thinking about was seeing Papa again. Just knowing she was in the same town as he was made her smile.

"When will we have our two dollars?" Mickey Duff blurted out. He was standing on the towpath looking worried that someone might steal *his* money.

"Now isn't tha time —" Billy Black began to say.

"We've done as we promised," stated Duff, "so they should pay as promised."

"Mrs. Haggrety here has more important matters ta concern herself with. . . ."

"No need, Mr. Black," Momma said, giving Duff a brittle stare. "We'll settle up with Mr. Duff and anyone else who wants his money. Maggie, get the tin and pay these men, then come along." Momma marched up a street that led into the heart of New Boston, Eamon at her side.

Maggie hurried down into the cabin. Her hands were shaking as she lifted the small box from under her covers. Soon she would see her papa again.

She emerged with the box under her arm and stepped from the *Betty* to the brown freighter, then down that boat's boarding plank to the towpath. She told herself to be as calm as she could as she opened the lid and took out two dollars. "Here is your money, Mr Duff, and thank you for your labors." Those were very nearly the words Uncle Hen used when paying men who'd helped them with cargo. "Does anyone else want to be paid now?"

"I can wait, miss," said Dick. His refusal was echoed by all the other men.

"Tha young lady is too polite ta say so," Billy Black told Duff, "but you can be off now and good riddance."

"That's not fair. . . ." Duff protested.

"Even a mule would know she didn't need to be bothered now," Dick said. "You'd best move along."

"Dick's right," Billy Black said. He took Duff by the arm and spun him around to face downstream. "The wisest thing is fer you ta wander off and not look back." Billy Black pointed down the towpath. "And may tha Lord forgive ya yer sins."

Mickey Duff looked around at the men glaring at him, mumbled a feeble cuss, then did as told, walking away meekly with his hands in his pockets.

Maggie was about to sprint off after her mother and brother, when she hesitated, the money tin suddenly feeling big and clumsy in her arms. What exactly was she afraid of, she asked herself, as she glanced around at Billy's Black's men. They might be a bit rough-looking, but they'd worked as hard as any crew without complaint or problem. And sometimes, as Billy Black might say, you have to have faith. "I'll just put this tin back and be on my way," she said, heading up the plank.

"Not to worry, Miss," Billy Black said when she reemerged a few moments later, "we'll leave a man here to watch over things."

"Thank you, Mr. Black," Maggie called as she hurried off. Three blocks later she came even with Momma.

"No need to run," her momma said sharply. Momma was walking at a steady, deliberate pace, head held high, eyes forward, lips set firmly. Her old self had returned. And that meant no sign of weakness, no hint of panic. "Don't slouch, Eamon," she cautioned, reaching for his hand. "We've nothing to be ashamed of."

The way Momma had taken Eamon's hand and not hers brought back Maggie's old feeling of being pushed away, the line between them slowing playing out.

She tried to think about Papa and Hen and how much she missed them, that she would see them in just a few minutes, but it still couldn't stop her from feeling hurt.

Just a few days ago, Maggie might have walked along helplessly as the feeling intensified. But now, after all she'd been through and done, after they'd all worked so hard together, Maggie knew she had to do something, no matter how Momma would react. She walked along for several steps, then did the only thing she could think of. She reached and took hold of her mother's other hand.

"I expect everyone is at the church," Momma announced, trying to sound in control. Then Momma looked around at Maggie, her eyes sad and worried, and returned the squeeze.

As soon as the church came into view, they saw the crowd, a dark mass that stretched from the open church doors and down the steps to the street. Every so often a man at the door would turn to make an announcement to the gathering. "Judge Bradley's looking at a list Mr. Rivington has presented to the court and frowning."

Maggie, Momma, and Eamon were close enough to hear the crowd murmuring, as if something important had just taken place. Familiar voices drew her attention and she spotted the Herkimer kids to the side, pointing at her and shouting, "Stupid ugly canal girl." She felt her heart start to pump, then noticed the angry bruise under the tallest boy's left eye. Maybe Abel had said hi for her like he'd promised.

"What's going on, Momma?" Eamon asked nervously.

"We'll know soon enough," she said as they came to the rear of the crowd. "Excuse me, sir, we need to get through."

The man looked around, annoyed, saw Momma's stern look, and immediately stepped aside, taking his hat off as he did. "Yes, ma'am. Hey," he called sharply to those in front, "this is Haggarty's wife and kids. Make way, do you hear, make way."

A narrow path opened and Momma, Eamon, and Maggie proceeded single file through the mass of bodies. Several people knew Momma and said hello, while some others mumbled about ridding the Canal of brawlers and other riffraff. It was hard for Maggie to tell if more people were for or against her papa and Uncle Hen.

Billy Black came hurrying up behind them, saying, "I'm with the family."

"He's shaking his head now," the man at the door announced. "He's looking at the second page and doesn't like what he's reading one bit."

Momma pushed into the church and a wave of warm, dead air made Maggie's head swim. Sweat began trickling from her brow as they wiggled their way up a side aisle until the crowd was so thickly packed, there was no room to move even an inch.

Maggie craned her neck as she searched for Papa. She assumed he would be at the front, but there were too many heads in her way, too many hats being waved back and forth as fans, for her to find him in the crowd.

Sheriff Einhornn stood at the front on the right side of the center aisle, his arms across his chest. A bitter taste filled Maggie's mouth when she saw his face. His three deputies were positioned at various spots in the church, each armed and looking very severe.

A man she took to be Judge Bradley was sitting at a small desk near the pulpit and facing the crowd, his white shirt buttoned all the way up. Behind him to the right, in the pews usually used by the choir, sat twelve jurors. Maggie hoped there was a canaler or two among them.

"Mr. Rivington," the judge said, taking his glasses off.

"There's Papa and Uncle Hen," Maggie whispered to Momma when Mr. Rivington, their lawyer, stood. Maggie was so happy she could barely contain her voice.

Both Papa and Uncle Hen were seated in small, wood chairs next to their lawyer and glancing around nervously. Clearly the trial had been going on a while, and Maggie wondered what had happened to worry her papa.

"Mr. Rivington," said Judge Bradley, "am I to understand that you intend to call all of these people as witnesses?" Maggie wouldn't say the judge looked angry, but he certainly didn't seem happy at the prospect of listening to so many people testify.

"Yes, Your Honor. And every one of them will tell you the same truth — that Tim and Henry Haggarty are good, honest men. . . ." Lawyer Rivington said more, but a smattering of applause mixed with some boos and whistles drowned out his words.

"Okay, okay," Judge Bradley growled, waving his gavel in the air to silence the crowd. He seemed tired or bored, it was hard to say which, and his eyes had heavy lines under them. "Settle down, everyone, so we can get on with this." He looked back at Lawyer Rivington. "So all of these folk . . . let's see" — he put his glasses on, glanced at the list, then removed his glasses to talk — "I take it these sixty-seven people will all be character witnesses for the defendants?"

"Yes, Your Honor. Sixty-seven of the state's finest citizens. Though we could have had a hundred! Two hundred even! Why, the defense could have called every lockkeeper, every —"

"A simple 'yes' will be enough." He waited for the ripple of laughter to die down. "We've already heard Captain Merritt's testimony. He told the Court how honorable both men are and how fair, especially in a fight. That neither one has ever thrown a dishonest punch or taken advantage of a helpless opponent, no matter how much that man deserved to be . . . what was the phrase Captain Merritt used?" — once again he put on his glasses — "deserved to be 'whooped senseless and stomped a few times.' Am I correct?"

"That is a fair if concise summary, Your Honor."

"And am I correct in thinking that everyone else on this list will say more or less the same thing about the defendants?"

"Each and every man and woman we intend to call

has had personal encounters with my clients. . . ." Judge Bradley scowled at Lawyer Rivington, which caused the man to break off his speech and gulp loudly. "Ah, yes, more or less, Your Honor."

"And will any of these folk say plain out they have material proof that these men are innocent of the crime charged?"

"Well, no, Your Honor. But their combined voices will be a powerful testament. . . ."

Judge Bradley inhaled slowly. "Heaven help your clients if they're paying you by the word, Mr. Rivington."

The crowd exploded into whoops and whistles and catcalls, and Maggie suddenly wanted to shout at everyone for making fun of Papa's lawyer, and at the judge for being so cruel. She remembered the angry look the man clearing the land had given her, and for no other reason than she was a canaler. Maybe the judge was related to him.

It took a minute or so before the crowd settled down enough for the trial to continue. "To speed these proceedings along, I propose to read out the names one at a time. Each person can stand where they are and say yes or no that they agree with Captain Merritt's testimony."

"Your Honor," Lawyer Rivington began to protest.

"Yes, yes, your objection is duly noted and overruled.

You can sit down now, Mr. Rivington." Judge Bradley turned to a man sitting in the pew across from Papa's lawyer. "Mr. Slater, does the State object to this summary or want to question any of these witnesses?"

A somewhat plump man of middling height with thick black hair stood. "The prosecution has no objections and no questions, Your Honor."

"Good," the judge said, obviously relieved. "Alright, let me see" — on went his glasses as he studied the paper — "Retired Captain Joshua Pettijohn."

"Here," Mr. Pettijohn called out from the other side of the church as he stood up. So Mr. Pettijohn had untied the *Bonanza* after five years of inaction and sailed down just to testify for her papa.

"Do you agree with my summary of these two men's characters, Mr. Pettijohn?"

"I do, but I want to add that I've seen Tim Haggarty in a tussle or two. . . ."

"Mr. Pettijohn." For the first time, the judge banged his gavel down, to get Mr. Pettijohn's attention. "Unless you have something new to add, this court doesn't need to hear any more praise for the defendants."

"Only that my wife, Esther, agrees and wants to be on record, too."

"Yes, Your Honor," Esther shouted, jumping to her feet. "These are sweet and honorable men, and anybody who says different is a bold-faced liar."

There was more laughter and even Judge Bradley had to smile. "Okay, Mrs. Pettijohn. I'll add your name to the list." He found a pencil and wrote it down. "Next is Sebastian Mutcher, lockkeeper at number forty-seven in Syracuse. Do you agree with my summary?"

"Yes, sir, I do and more so. I've never had a lick of trouble from Captain Tim. . . ."

"That'll do, Mr. Mutcher. Next is . . ."

"This isn't fair, Momma," Maggie said in a whisper. "Why won't he let Papa's friends talk?"

"I don't know," Momma said.

"I'd make him listen if it was me trying to talk," Eamon said, loud enough that Sheriff Einhornn frowned in their direction.

Maggie might have said something to her brother except that she saw her momma wince and grab hold of the church pew next to her.

"You okay, Momma?" Maggie asked.

"I'll be fine. It's just this stifling air."

A man sitting next to Maggie noticed Momma for the first time and leaped to his feet to give her his seat. "Sorry I didn't see you before, ma'am." He jabbed the shoulder of the man next to him, who also got up so she, Momma, and Eamon could all squeeze in together. "He's not the easiest of judges," the first man added, "but some who've had dealings with him say he's fair enough."

"Let's hope so," Momma replied as she sat down. "Thank you for giving up your seat."

The calling of names went on for thirty long minutes — Captain James Hammil of the *Corinth*, out of Buffalo, Mrs. Priscilla Hobberman from Port Byron, Una Fluke, lockkeeper at number 53 in Clyde.

The man at the door called out each name for the crowd and said "yes" afterward, which was followed by a rumble from his audience. Whenever the noise seemed particularly unfriendly, Maggie hoped the jury wasn't listening.

The names flowed along — Captain Enos Throop, Mr. Bernhard Bauer, butcher and iceman from Camillus. For Maggie, the biggest surprise came when the name Jozina Wittick Dalrumple was called and Jozie rose up as tall and straight as a pine tree.

"Do you agree with my summary of . . ."

"No, sir," she barked before he could finish, "not at all." A ripple of excitement pulsed through the church, and from those outside when the man at the door shouted, "She said no!"

"Quiet, everybody," the judge said, banging his gavel

down hard. "Quiet. This is a court of law, not a saloon!" That got the attention of most people and the rumble settled down, though there was still a great deal of noise from outside. "You don't agree with my summary, Mrs. Dalrumple?"

"I don't agree with your words, Judge, with all due respect. I would say that it is impossible that either Tim Haggarty or Henry Haggarty could ever stoop to hitting anyone from behind under any circumstances and that anyone who thinks so needs his head examined. Which is exactly what I told your sheriff there."

The cheer that went up was surprisingly loud and very nearly drowned out the impatient hammering of the judge's gavel. Jozie sat down trying to look very serious, though Maggie was sure a smile was dancing at the corner of her lips.

"Okay, quiet. Quiet, please! Now that we have that out of the way" — he looked over the top of his glasses at Jozie, to which she nodded — "Mr. Slater. Does the State have anything further to add to its case?"

"The court has already heard Captain John Forster state that one of the defendants threatened Russell Ackroyd," the prosecutor said. It took a second for Maggie to realize he was referring to Long-fingered John, who was sitting only a few pews in front of them along with his men. "We've also heard Sheriff Einhornn describe the bruises on the defendant's right hand. In our opinion, Your Honor, the circumstances paint a grim picture for the defendants and are sufficient for a conviction."

A murmur of approval greeted the prosecutor's closing. When they'd quieted, the judge cleared his throat. "This certainly does look bad for the defendants. . . ."

Lawyer Rivington leaped to his feet. "But the defense hasn't rested its case, Judge Bradley! We intend to show that all of this evidence when looked at fairly —"

"Mr. Rivington," the judge snapped, "will you please shut up so the Court can speak!"

"Your Honor, this is all circumstantial —"

"Sit down, Mr. Rivington, or I'll hold you in contempt. . . ."

At Lawyer Rivington's objection, the crowd had come alive again, many shouting in agreement, others calling for justice and long prison terms. Several arguments broke out among the crowd as Judge Bradley repeatedly slammed his gavel upon the table.

The judge continued speaking even before order was completely restored, so no matter how hard Maggie listened, all she heard was a great mumble of indecipherable words. One phrase, however, did jump through the noise to chill her blood. "I agree with the prosecution," he said, though the commotion in the church again rose to drown out the rest of the sentence as Lawyer Rivington raised another objection.

Momma squeezed Maggie's hand hard, as if she were holding on for dear life.

"He can't do that to Papa and Uncle Hen!" Maggie shouted to her momma.

Judge Bradley stood and banged his gavel down several times. There was another wave of loud protests, but eventually the rumblings subsided. The judge wiped the perspiration from his face before he spoke again. "I'll remind you, this is not only a court of law, but a church of the Lord, so behave yourselves accordingly." He took his seat and began putting the papers on his desk in order.

Don't play with those silly papers, Maggie thought, and when he still didn't say anything, she said out loud, "Why doesn't he stop dawdling?"

Judge Bradley glanced in her direction and frowned. "As I was saying," he began after clearing his throat, "I agree with the prosecution that this *looks* bad. But looking bad isn't enough, especially when you have two men who have been called fair dealing by everyone. Even Captain Forster admitted he was a clean fighter."

"But what about the victim, Your Honor?" the prose-cutor asked. "Russell Ackroyd is in a hotel nearby, still unconscious. . . ."

"And if he could wake long enough to point a finger at either of these men, that would be enough for me. But he can't and I'm not about to send this to the jury on such slim evidence, Mr. Slater. I therefore declare this a mistrial." The judge banged the gavel.

Cheering drowned out the rest of what he was saying, and then Papa leaped to his feet, whooping loudly and hugging Hen.

"We won!" Maggie shouted, as she, Eamon, and Momma embraced and jumped up and down. "We *won!*"

The crowd inside the church was already in motion, some heading toward the front to congratulate Papa, Henry, and their lawyer, and even Judge Bradley, while others made their way to the nearest door, everybody talking excitedly. Maggie saw Long-fingered John shove his way ahead of several men to get to the exit.

"Come along," Momma told them as she began moving toward the center aisle. "We need to get Papa and Uncle Hen a decent meal."

"Papa!" Eamon shouted. He climbed up on the pew seat and began waving both arms in the air. "Papa, over here!"

Maggie got on her tiptoes but couldn't see past

the wide hat of a woman in front of her. "Here, miss. Let me give ya a hand up," said Billy Black as he took her elbow to help her step up onto the pew beside her brother.

"Papa, Papa!" Eamon jumped up and down. "Here we are, Papa!"

Maggie waved as well when Papa spotted them. He broke free from the man who was excitedly pumping his hand and began making his way toward them.

"Maggie and Eamon, get down from there this instant," Momma ordered.

"I think tha Lord would understand, Ma'am," Billy Black said to Maggie, just as the church bell began to ring. "And listen ta that," Billy Black added, looking heavenward. "He certainly has a way of making His opinion clear."

Maggie was about to reply when something caught her eye and made her look up. He was standing in the side aisle, only a few feet from where she had been minutes before. The only one in the entire church not moving to an exit, the only one not shaking someone's hand or chatting away. He was looking right at her and smiling. And this time Maggie knew for certain. Michael Connelly's smile was just for her.

Thirsting for 21
Blood

Maggie was about to smile back at Michael Connelly when Eamon yanked her hand and sent her flying off the pew toward the center aisle. She glanced back once, but Michael had already been swallowed up by the crowd.

"Eamon!"

"Come on," he called over his shoulder. "There's Papa!"

Impatiently, Momma plowed through the swarming people with her children just behind. Next, they were embracing Papa and Uncle Henry in a tangle of arms. The hug felt so good, Maggie wanted it to go on forever.

"Oh, I missed you all so much," Papa said with obvious relief. "That sheriff was looking to lock us up for good."

"Every time he brought our food," Hen added, "he waved that gun of his around and said, 'No funny business from you two.' Course, Tim was always practicing boxing in the cell, so I guess I can't blame the man."

They embraced again, but then Papa suddenly pulled

away. "The shipment," he blurted out. "Did you get it to Tucker's on time?"

"It was tight," Momma said proudly, "but we did it! And Maggie collected the bonus."

"We certainly have a lot to celebrate," Papa said. "Let's get out of here."

It seemed to take forever after this to get out of the church and into the fresh air and sunshine. Lawyer Rivington appeared and was paid and there were more people congratulating Papa and Hen or thanking them for past kindnesses.

"I thought I'd never find you in this mob," said Jozie, pushing through the crowd to get to Maggie and her family. She hugged and congratulated Papa and Hen, then she kissed Momma. "Was worried you were caught up in that Lockport mess and didn't make it."

"We were," Momma started to explain, "but Mr. Black here . . ." She looked around, confused. "He was just here," she said. "He got us through Lockport and back here."

Maggie searched for Billy Black, too, but once again he'd disappeared. And she hadn't even paid him and his friends their two dollars for helping them.

The little group was heading toward the Canal when, suddenly, a booming voice called out from the front door of a saloon. "You escaped the hangman, mick. No denying yer a clever one."

It was Long-fingered John and his crew, along with a gaggle of other men, including the orange-haired captain. Maggie spotted the captain of the *Quick City*, too, his nose a livid purple-red where Momma had punched it. Her heart pounding, Maggie searched quickly for Michael Connelly, but didn't see him.

John downed what was left of his whiskey and handed the empty glass to one of his pals. "Helped out by a clown of a judge" — his eyes locked onto Papa — "and a few dollars, no doubt."

"Nothing dishonest was done," Hen said, facing the Canadian. "Simple justice for innocent men."

"Justice bought and paid for!" Long-fingered John's gray-black eyes flashed a challenge.

"We've no fight with you," Papa said at last. To his group Papa added, "Come along, Hen. Now isn't the time."

"Watch him slither away," the Canadian called after him.

"Shut up, you big, stupid dumb ox," Eamon screamed. He charged at Long-fingered John, but Hen grabbed the back of his shirt and held him in place. Stopped in his attack, Eamon continued yelling at the Canadian.

"That's how they baited Russell." John's teeth gleamed as he gave a big grin. "A real team, they are."

"Don't you go and listen to that one," Jozie said to Papa in a soothing voice. "He hasn't the brains of a canal barge."

"And another comes to his rescue," the Canadian announced loudly. "First it was the judge, then the boy, and now an old woman. . . ."

"You've no call to say that to Jozie," Momma said.

"And the wife!" Long-fingered John continued. "Who's next? This one?" — he nodded dismissively in Hen's direction — "or the girl? Maybe one of the mules?"

"There's no need for this," Papa told Long-fingered John. "We want to get to our boat, so why don't you and your friends . . ."

"Listen to him," Long-fingered John said sarcastically. "Wants to hide in his boat. That beatin' he gave Russell musta took all the fight outta him." He paused dramatically before adding, "Go on with ya, then, mick. Run off to yer boat."

Maggie saw Papa's back stiffen, his teeth clamping down so tight his jaw pulsed. Then in disgust Papa turned. "Let's go, Anna. Jozie." He waited until they each joined him and they continued down the street again.

An uneasy chill gripped Maggie. Papa was letting

that man insult him, and in front of this crowd. What was wrong with him?

"There he goes," the Canadian sang out, finally coming to a stop. "If he won't fight for his honor, maybe he'll fight for his money. Or is he too much of a coward?"

"Tim, let's keep going," Momma said.

"He's all hot air and guff. . . ." Jozie added.

"Keep quiet, you old cow!" the Canadian roared.

Papa suddenly stopped walking and carefully disengaged his hold on both Momma and Jozie. He faced Long-fingered John and gave him a long, cool appraisal. A strange hush suddenly dropped down on everyone there. "You've no place to say that to Jozie."

"I'll say what I want when I want." Long-fingered John glanced around at his audience, clearly enjoying himself. "Or are you going to stop me?"

"If I need to."

It was as if lightning had struck the middle of the street. A collective gasp rippled through the onlookers as everyone quickstepped backward to avoid being singed. Men shouted to alert others that a fight was about to commence and one man crowed giddily, "It's going to be a dilly of a tumble, let me tell you. A real dilly."

"You can beat'm, Papa," Eamon was shouting. "You can whup'm."

Momma's face had tightened in disapproval. "Tim," she said. Jozie took her arm and gently tugged her back from Papa. She glared in Long-fingered John's direction, before adding, "Tim, be careful."

"Papa!" Maggie squeaked. She was going to say more, but an image flashed before her eyes and blotted out the rest of her words, a single still picture of Papa sprawled on the ground, face bloodied, arms flung out awkwardly, their hard-earned bonus lost. As the familiar numb feeling invaded her, she went to stand near her momma.

"If you're ready," Papa said to his opponent as he moved forward.

"Not so fast, mick," Long-fingered John replied. "I aim to have my bonus early this season. So how much is it to be?"

Papa relaxed his fists, letting his arms drop. "This isn't about the money. . . ."

"One hundred?" Long-fingered John persisted. "Two hundred? How much did I take from you last time? Three hundred?"

"Three hundred and forty dollars," Papa answered. "Plus fifty from Henry."

The Canadian laughed hard, clutching his belly. "So this isn't about the money, huh? But you remember to the penny, don't you?"

Papa raised his fists and took a few tentative steps toward his opponent. "Can we cover that, Anna?"

Momma's lips were fixed in a straight, hard line. It was clear she was furious, though Maggie wasn't sure if she was furious at Long-fingered John or Papa. Probably both. "Tim, we've only enough to pay back the loan. . . ."

"I'll add my second team to make up the difference," Papa said to Long-fingered John.

"That mismatched pair isn't worth the iron in their hooves."

"Rudy and Tom are the best pullers on the Canal!" Maggie found herself yelling. "They pulled our boat for hours and never gave up. They have heart."

There was another roar of laughter from Long-fingered John. "Yet another Haggarty heard from, and did you hear what this one said? 'They have heart.'" Long-fingered John laughed out loud again, laughed at her silly words, laughed to mock her. . . .

"My two lead mules as well," Papa added.

Tears filled Maggie's eyes. Papa couldn't bet all their mules.

Long-fingered John considered the bet, then smiled. "Let's stop playing around, mick. My boat, gear, and mules for yours, plus whatever cash you have."

"Tim, don't you dare," Momma warned. "If . . ."

"Agreed," Papa said firmly.

Momma's face turned scarlet in rage and she would have said more, only she knew the rule of the Canal. Once spoken, the bet couldn't be withdrawn.

A few seconds was all it had taken. Passions had flared in that brief time, and reason had disappeared like a stone tossed into the Canal. Now everything they owned, everything they had worked so hard to save these past days, was once again riding on Papa's fists.

"Now let's get to it," Long-fingered John said. He took a step toward Papa, pausing long enough to grab a whiskey from one of his pals, drain it, and hand back the glass. Up went his fists.

That was when Maggie remembered the baby. "Papa, don't do it!" she cried out, grabbing his shirtsleeve and tugging. "You can't!"

"Maggie, let go." He shook her hand loose. "You know better. . . ."

"Well, mick, I'm waitin'."

Papa gazed into Maggie's eyes, then to his wife's, then back to Maggie's. She saw it again. The look he'd given her just before he'd been knocked senseless. I've no choice, he'd tried to tell her. I don't want to fight anymore, but there's no one else. He touched a finger to

Maggie's shoulder. "Go stand with your momma there," he said softly, "while I take care of this."

Papa took his fighting stance again, his body leaning forward and turned at a slight angle to his opponent, his fists high up to protect his chin. As the men began cautiously circling each other, the crowd scurried back farther and began calling encouragement to their favorite.

"Watch that left of his, Tim," Hen shouted. "Remember what we talked about."

"Get'm, John," the orange-haired man called. "One right and he'll drop like a rock."

"Stop dancing and start fighting," another man shouted. "I've ten says an Irishman can whip a Canadian any day."

Long-fingered John took several deliberate steps forward and threw the first punch, which grazed Papa's arm, and a second, which Tim knocked aside an inch or so before it got to his face. Papa leaned back, ducked to his right as another punch flicked his way.

"Keep moving, Tim," Jozie yelled. "Don't let'm get in tight to you."

More circling followed and both men threw several tentative punches. Sweat was dripping down Papa's face and into his eyes where it stung and made seeing difficult. He was wiping it away when Long-fingered John gave a loud bellow and rushed forward, fists pumping. This time Papa stood his ground, blocked a right hand, was clipped on the ear with the left before he could land several punches of his own. Maggie heard the rapid *pop-popping* of fists striking flesh, the men's grunts, and the crowd's wild cheer.

Papa blocked one of John's rights and countered with a left overhand that landed on the Canadian's right shoulder. The blow was strong enough to force the man back two steps but not enough to knock him to the ground. In fact, Long-fingered John dropped his fists and stood tall, a leering smile on his face.

"That was it, mick? That punch was all you got?" His smile was replaced by a malicious grin. "Oh, this is going to be fun. . . ."

Papa took several deep breaths. A thin line of blood trickled from his ear onto his neck, where it mixed with his sweat to blossom into a grotesque crimson blotch. He seemed older to Maggie, older and unsure.

"He's scared, Papa," Eamon taunted. "He's scared, he's scared, he's scared."

Long-fingered John scowled at Eamon, spit on the ground, and raised his fists. "Scared of a dumb potato eater," he snarled as he marched toward Papa. "That'll be the day!"

There was another cheer from the crowd, savage and cruel and thirsting for more blood as the two men came together and another flurry of punches was thrown.

A tingling sadness ran through Maggie's head as the men fought, clinched arms, pushed away, and fought some more. Then the old feeling returned to her. The feeling that she had to get away. This was the part of the Canal she needed to escape, had to escape. Not her silly brother, not her parents, not even the slow, still water and boring routine. She wanted to be away from this brutal hard edge that turned people into a cheering mob, that put Papa and their livelihood at risk. But where could she go when life on land, life at the far end of the alley or some distant exotic city, seemed just as foreign and dangerous?

Long-fingered John connected with a right that staggered Papa, but his left missed wide as Papa wiggled to the side. Papa shook his head to throw off a shower of sweat and blood and danced about as the Canadian swung again and missed.

He's tired, Maggie realized. Long-fingered John is tired or drunk or both. And Papa still has some bounce in his legs.

It was a left jab to the chin that set the Canadian

back on his heels, and a right to his belly that made him expel a great whoosh of air. A dazed expression passed across Long-fingered John's face, and then Papa's right fist caught him square on the nose.

Maggie winced at the spray of blood and at the big man's helpless groan. His legs wobbled as he took a step to the side, then they buckled, sending him crashing to the muddy street. Instinct had the man rolling over and trying to get up almost immediately, just as her papa had tried last November. His feeble, clumsy movements, the way his head hung down as if held on by twine, said Long-fingered John was finished, the fight over.

Instantly, the crowd surged forward to close in around the two fighters, some settling bets, others jabbering away about the fight.

"Grab ahold of him," the orange-haired man ordered two of his crew, nodding toward the groaning Canadian, "and let's get outta here."

"Not before he settles his bet," Papa said. He was exhausted, his face bloodied, but that didn't stop Papa from standing as tall as he could, poised for any additional action that might be needed. Hen came up next to him, still holding tight to Eamon.

"Was a fair fight and you'll settle the bets," Captain

Merritt said, stepping from the crowd. "Who agrees with me?"

"I do," said Dick. He pointed at one of Long-fingered John's men. "You owe me five dollars, so don't think you can run out on it!" The other members of Billy Black's crew were right next to him.

Just as one after another had called their good wishes to Momma at Lockport, men came forward to back up Tim Haggarty and his brother until the orange-haired man and his friends were outnumbered and entirely encircled. Maggie noticed that one of those joining her papa's side was Michael Connelly.

"Should have stood up to them long ago," Jozie said.

"You're all very brave now," the orange-haired man said, "but wait till John here is up again. . . ."

"Stop flapping your lips and get him on his feet," Papa ordered. "There's some business to settle." Papa surveyed the men around him. "And when that's done, I'm sure we can find a suitable way to celebrate the occasion."

A cheer erupted, accompanied by more shouts. Long-fingered John's pals got him to his feet and began leading him toward the Canal.

"Tim Haggarty," Momma said very sternly, "you have a lot of explaining to do before you start in celebrating. . . ."

Papa hunched his shoulders like a naughty child.

The crowd was drifting toward the Canal, with Long-fingered John being supported between two of his followers and awake enough to mumble that he wanted to continue the fight. Maggie spotted Michael Connelly standing by himself to the side.

"Are you coming along?" Maggie asked.

"Well, miss," he said with an easy, backwoods twang. "I'm not sure I'd be welcome, being I was a part of that *Quick City* crew."

"You stood by my papa when he needed you," Maggie answered. She looked square into his startlingly blue eyes. "My name is Maggie," she said. "Maggie Haggarty."

Michael Connelly whipped his hat off and raked his hair flat. "Knew that the first time I saw you, miss," he said shyly. "Why, everybody up and down the whole Erie Canal knows about you and your family."

Maggie felt the color rising in her cheeks, accompanied by a shy smile.

"Come on then," she said. "We have some celebrating to do."

A Big World 22
out There

Long-fingered John was brought to the towpath next to his boat and seated on a kitchen chair. A pail of cold Erie water was dumped over his head to revive him, which produced a great deal of sputtering and some mumbled cusses. When he revived enough to know where he was, a plank of wood was placed on his lap.

"You need to sign this," Hen told him, putting a piece of paper on the plank, "in case you or your friends here have any funny business on your minds. It says, 'I swear before God and these witnesses that I lost to Tim Haggarty in a fair fight.' Sign at the bottom." Hen handed Long-fingered John a pencil and pointed to the paper.

"You stopped the fight too soon," John mumbled. His nose wasn't bleeding much anymore, but a few drops still plopped down onto the paper.

"You lost the fight," someone in the crowd suggested, "so sign the paper and get moving."

Long-fingered John signed his name, as did every

member of his crew. Several men from Papa's side also signed as witnesses.

"Well, she's yours," mumbled Long-fingered John, gesturing toward his boat.

"Don't want your old scow," Papa said. "Or your mules or gear, either. Just want my money back."

"What?" the Canadian said, not understanding.

"The three hundred and ninety dollars from the first fight," Papa said slowly, as if he was talking to a child. "That's all I want from you."

Long-fingered John stared at Maggie's father for a long time and then it seemed to dawn on him. "Just the cash? You don't want my boat or mules?"

"That's right," Papa said. "And you can count yourself lucky."

Maggie found herself filling with pride. Papa had beaten the Canadian fairly and soundly. No one would have blamed him if he took everything from the man, but he still wouldn't take advantage of a defeated opponent, not even one as mean and cussed as Long-fingered John.

Long-fingered John counted out three hundred and ninety dollars and handed it to Papa. "Next time . . ." he muttered unsteadily as he pointed a threatening finger at Papa, then seemed to lose his thought as a new and more important one came to him. "Well, boys," he said, pushing himself clumsily to his feet. "I've enough cash left to buy us a round or two, so let's get to it." And Long-fingered John, the orange-haired man, and the rest of their crew wandered off.

Right after this, Momma started in on Papa. "You're not out of jail two minutes and you're in a brawl!"

"I tried to steer clear of it, honey, honest I did. You saw me at Jozie's. Even back there in the street. Was him that pushed me and insulted Jozie. He forced me into it."

"And you bet like a drunken sailor," Momma snapped. "After what happened last year and everything we went through because of that! What were you thinking?"

"Ah, Anna," Papa pleaded, "I admit I got carried away and lost my head. . . ."

"You could have lost our boat and mules, and then where would we be?" she demanded. "And with another baby on the way!"

Papa gulped back whatever he was about to say and looked so startled you might have thought he'd swallowed an apple whole. "A baby!" he managed to gasp. "You mean you're . . . we're . . . a baby?"

"Yes." Momma seemed as startled by the abruptness of her announcement as Papa, but after a moment she recovered. "And I won't have you putting your family's future in jeopardy again, Tim Haggarty." She poked her finger against his chest. "This was positively, absolutely your last fight ever. Am I clear?"

"A baby," Papa repeated. He smiled proudly and looked at Uncle Hen. "Hen, did you hear that? We're having another baby."

"Congratulations," Hen said. He moved to give Anna a hug, but she held up her hand to stop him.

"Not until he promises," she said. "And means it." She faced Papa and waited, arms folded across her chest, her eyes locked onto his. Everyone around them grew still.

"Well," Papa said quietly. Then he cleared his throat and added more loudly, "With the Lord and everyone here as witness, I swear that this was my last fight ever. So help me."

There was a muffled cheer from those closest and a voice called out, "We'll see that he keeps his word, Mrs. Haggarty." Momma smiled at that and accepted the congratulations that followed.

After this, everyone made their way to the *Betty*, where the tarp was removed from the empty cargo hold and the party that followed went long into the night, with several toasts and much singing, some of it on key. Eamon spent a great deal of time boasting that he could have whupped Long-fingered John and his entire crew single-handed, while Jozie spun one long yarn after another.

Maggie paid Dick and the other men their two dollars. When she finished, she couldn't find Michael Connelly in the crowd and for an instant worried that he'd wandered out of her life again. She breathed a sigh of relief when she spotted him over near the fiddle player.

"Your family sure has a lot of friends," Michael said when Maggie came up to him. "Must be nice knowing you can count on so many people."

"I guess we're lucky that way. We wouldn't have made the bonus without a lot of help." A brief, shy silence followed until Maggie recalled that day's fight and realized something. "You don't have a job anymore, do you? Because you stood with Papa."

Michael shrugged. "Ah, doesn't much matter," he said easily. "Anyway, I never could fit into those tiny bunks without bumping my head. At least on my daddy's farm, I could stretch out on my bed."

She almost didn't want to ask, afraid of what the answer might be, but she did anyway. "So, you'll be leaving the Canal?"

"Leaving!" Michael looked downright shocked by

the notion. "No. Thought I'd look for a job along the water here." He gestured up the towpath toward a line of stores and factories. "Plenty of places could use help, I reckon."

"That's true!" Maggie answered so loudly, it startled her and made her giggle nervously. "At least I'll know where to find you," she said in a quieter voice. "That is, if you let me know where you are." She felt herself blushing at her boldness.

"Oh, you'll know where I am," Michael replied, and even in the dim light, Maggie was certain he blushed, too.

When Captain Merritt came over to chat with Michael, Maggie went to the towpath to find Papa. She felt light-headed and giddy, wondering if this was what love felt like. She reached Papa just as Billy Black appeared, a folded piece of paper in his hand.

"Cap'n Haggrety," Billy announced. "I'm Billy Black, and —"

"Mr. Black!" Papa blurted out. He grabbed Billy Black's hand and pumped it hard. "Anna told me what you did for us. How you got us through Lockport and to Tucker's. We would've lost our boat if it wasn't for you and your friends."

"'Twas tha Lord saved tha day," Billy said. "And yer family."

"And the mules," Maggie couldn't help adding.

"And the mules," Billy Black agreed, his face breaking

into a smile. "But I'm here now on another matter, Mr. Haggrety." He took a folded piece of paper from his pocket and handed it to Papa. "Judge Bradley asked that I give this ta ya."

"Judge Bradley?" Papa said nervously. He seemed reluctant to take the paper.

"Was there when tha judge wrote it," Billy Black said. "Says that Russell Ackroyd woke up and declared without a doubt that neither Cap'n Haggrety or his brother ever laid a hand ta him. Was a couple of thugs from another boat at tha tavern tryin' ta settle an ol' score. Seems Russell's mouth has earned him any number of enemies along tha Canal."

"He just woke up?" Maggie asked.

"He had some help, miss. Ya see, I bumped inta that nice Mr. Bauer, and him and his love of ice put me in mind of something I once heard. We got chunks of ice from his boat and put'm all around Russell's body. Ten minutes later and he was a-shiverin'. Twenty minutes and he turned blue. Tha sheriff about stopped tha whole thing, but then Russell opened his eyes and started in cussing loud as a stuck pig. It's going ta take a better man than me ta save that one."

"You brought him back to life like the horse!" Maggie said.

"He would have come 'round sooner or later." Billy Black smiled. "We just speeded tha man along, is all."

"Whatever you did," Papa said, "we appreciate. You'll stay a while to help us celebrate all our good fortune?"

"That's a fine offer and I thank ya, but I'm not tha drinkin' kind anymore. Best ta avoid tha temptation." Before Papa could protest, Billy Black added, "Besides, my work here is done and I need ta get home. Never know when tha Lord might summon me again. But I do have a favor ta ask of ya, if I might."

"Anything," Papa said.

"If ya know of someone needing a captain and crew, could ya put in a good word fer Dick and some of t'others that come down with us? They're good men at heart and I'd appreciate it."

"We'll spread the word, Mr. Black," Papa said. "It's the least we can do."

"That's all I ask," Billy Black said. He shook hands again with Papa and said good night. Next he shook hands with Maggie. "Want ta say thanks, miss, fer givin' this ol' sinner a chance at salvation."

Maggie found the compliment embarrassing and had to look down at the towpath. "But I didn't want your help at first. . . ."

"And who could blame ya, tha way I barged in on yer

problems and went on about talkin' ta God." He laughed so hard, his crooked teeth glowed in the dark. "Ah, ya never let yer guard down and that's okay, that's smart. But ya trusted me enough ta give me a chance and that's the important thing. Most folk make their mind up and never budge an inch from there. They get stuck, but not you."

Billy Black said good-bye and headed upstream.

Maggie felt a sudden emptiness. A few days before, she was annoyed and frightened by him. Now she wasn't sure what a day would be like without Billy Black around. "Mr. Black," Maggie called out.

He turned and was about to say something, but before he could, Maggie planted a kiss on his bristly cheek. "Thank you again, Mr. Black."

"Till we meet again, miss," he said, before turning to wander up the towpath. Maggie noticed he was listing slightly to the right, but there was also a certain bounce to his step.

"He's" — Papa scratched his head — "unusual, isn't he?"

Maggie nodded. "He's very persistent."

"Funny, that's what Momma says about you." Papa sipped his cider. "She said you were the one who got the shipment to Tucker's on time, got us that bonus, and saved the boat."

"We had help," Maggie said, glancing to where Billy Black was disappearing into the dark.

"Momma said it was you who pushed her and Eamon and took care of the mules. Even made that new team decent pullers. She said you were as skilled as any captain on the Erie Canal. That's big praise coming from your momma." He paused and looked into Maggie's eyes. "Don't know anybody your age who could have done what you done, Maggie."

"Ah, Papa," Maggie said shyly, trying to hide her pleasure. "I only did what had to be done."

"And we're going to need you even more what with this baby on the way." He blinked his eyes as if seeing something for the very first time. "Lord, there's going to be a world of changes on this boat when that baby gets here. How are we ever going to manage?"

"We'll think of something," Maggie answered. "We always do."

Papa kissed Maggie on top of her head and went off to find Momma. Michael Connelly and Captain Merritt were still jawing away, so Maggie made her way to the stern deck by herself. Even with several lamps lit in the cargo area and a three-quarter moon overhead, it was dark back there and surprisingly calming.

She could just barely hear her papa's voice followed

by her momma's laughter. It was good that Momma was happy again and relaxed enough to laugh.

Eamon's higher-pitched voice sliced right between those of her parents. "I drove all day and all night so we could get back here for the trial. . . ."

Like a real canaler, Maggie thought. She had to smile at his little-boy bluster and at her own sense of contentment. They had pushed each other and the mules, overcoming one problem after another. They'd had help, of course. Billy Black and his friends. And all of the boaters at Lockport. Hundreds of people had come to their aid. The Canal was a real neighborhood, she realized, and as tight-knit and protective as any on land.

Papa began singing a song in the old language and several on board joined him. She didn't know the words by heart, but she remembered it was a song about people leaving Ireland and sailing to America, about what they left behind and what they hoped to find in their new home.

Maggie leaned back against the stern rail and listened — to the singing and clapping, to the water slapping at the bow, to the stillness in the night that went on forever. Tonight she didn't want to escape the Canal and her family to live on land. Oh, she would travel beyond the Big Ditch. Somehow she knew she would get to the big city to the south and maybe even other places farther away. But there was plenty of time for that in her future.

What she understood now was that she'd completed a great journey that couldn't be measured in miles traveled or dollars collected. She'd left behind one place in her life to step onto a new and mysterious path, one that stretched out in front of her like the great Erie Canal itself. What surprised her most was that she wasn't scared of what she might find along the way. She wasn't scared one little bit.

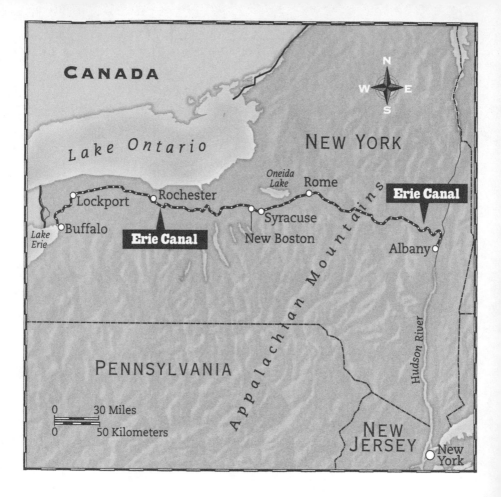

The Erie Canal allowed travel from the Great Lakes across New York State to Albany, and then south to New York City.

About the Erie Canal

At the beginning of the nineteenth century, Americans living in the thirteen original states were already looking to the west for new land to settle and farm. The problem was how to get thousands of people to the frontier, and how to get the products of their farms back to the eastern markets.

Most states chose to build new roads. Unfortunately, road tended to turn to muddy quagmires in spring, and cost a great deal of money to repair and maintain. Worse, it cost more than two dollars to ship a single barrel of flour 130 miles overland. The same barrel could travel 160 miles by water for only a quarter.

For legislators in New York, the answer to this situation seemed obvious. Instead of cutting new roads through their forests, they would create a 363-mile-long water route to connect the Hudson River with Lake Erie.

BUILDING A VAST WATERWAY

The reality of actually building this vast waterway was, to say the least, daunting. In addition to an elevation difference of more than 560 feet between Lake Erie and the Hudson, there were valleys, swamps, and mountains to cross with numerous

THE LOCK.

After this boat entered the lock, the downstream gates were closed by pushing on the long balance beams. Small doors, called sluices, in the upstream gates were then opened. Water would flood the lock until it was level with the upstream portion of the canal. Finally, the upstream gates were opened and the boat would go on its way.

fast-flowing rivers and streams in between. At the time, the building of the Erie Canal was going to be one of the greatest engineering feats in the history of the world.

To get the waterway up and down the uneven terrain, engineers designed eighty-three locks with lifts ranging from six to twelve feet. Eighteen stone aqueducts were constructed to get the forty-feet-wide and four-feet-deep canal across rivers and valleys. Laborers working for fifty cents a day blasted their way through granite mountains and shoveled out swamps, all the while battling mosquitoes, cold and rain, disease, and one another.

The task was so daunting that many people thought the entire undertaking was a waste of time and money. Thomas Jefferson, a man who distrusted cities and big government, thought the idea was sheer "madness." New York editor Mordecai Noah called the project a "monument of weakness and folly." As work on the Erie Canal crept along and costs topped seven million dollars, newspapers questioned the thinking of one of its chief proponents, New York governor DeWitt Clinton, and even began referring to it derisively as "Clinton's Ditch."

But forward the work went, year after year. From the time the first shovel of dirt was dug up on July 4, 1817, it would be eight years before the Erie Canal was declared officially complete. To the surprise of its many detractors, the Erie Canal proved to be an immediate and overwhelming success.

That first year, more than 13,000 boats were counted locking through one town and more than 40,000 passengers traveled on the new waterway. The Erie Canal was so successful (and profitable) that six additional canals would eventually be dug off of it to connect other areas of New York to expanding markets. Inspired by New York's success, many states rushed to build their own canals and America's Golden Age of Canals was launched.

Canals opened up areas of wilderness where roads were either very rough or nonexistent. They provided smooth, speedy service even though the fastest passenger packets rarely went more than four miles per hour. Despite the leisurely pace, the Erie Canal cut the traveling time between Albany and Buffalo in half (with a fast packet covering the distance in five to seven days) and became the first major "highway" for settlers heading into the untamed west.

CANAL PEOPLE

Most of the boats were owned, captained, and crewed by men, though women sometimes inherited boats when a husband or father died and simply carried on the business. Entire families traveled together, living, cooking, and sleeping in a cabin and sleeping cuddy that measured a total of ten feet by fourteen feet. Usually every member of the family would be assigned some sort of boat-related task, from caring for and driving the mules or horses, to steering the boat, depending on age and ability.

The canal was a rough place filled with its share of tough, brutal men. But the vast majority of people were decent, law abiding, and mannerly. The very narrowness of the canal itself also helped forge strong ties between canalers. There was a willingness to help others when a boat was damaged or when an individual or animal fell sick. Everyone understood the challenges and dangers of living and working on water and everyone knew that disaster could strike at any moment.

Canalers often encountered hostility from those who lived on land, especially during the canal's opening years. In order to build the canal, thousands of acres of land had to be seized by the state. Compensation for this land was modest and to exacerbate problems, dissatisfied farmers often found their land literally cut in half by water (which was why hundreds of small bridges had to be constructed). In addition, canalers were initially viewed as little better than uncouth, uneducated vagrants or unscrupulous ruffians.

As the Canal proved to be more and more successful and businesses and farmers saw sizable financial gains, attitudes about canalers began to soften. While some farmers and their children held on to grudges for years, real friendships began to develop between canal boat families and the folk who lived along the waterway.

AN ERA COMES TO AN END

The Golden Era of Canals lasted only a few decades. Competition in the form of railroads began appearing in the 1830s, and especially after the Civil War, when the transcontinental railroad united the East and West coasts.

There was no contest between the canals and railroads. Canals couldn't operate during the winter months; railroads could move goods and people all year round and thus could charge lower fares. Canals tried to compete by slashing tolls and freight rates, but it was a losing battle.

Canals began closing in the 1870s, but a few in areas not serviced by railroads were able to survive into the early twentieth century. Today only short stretches of the original Erie Canal are still used for transporting goods; the miles of waterway that remain are traveled mostly by tourists and outdoor water enthusiasts. The canaler's way of life that Maggie and her family experienced — a life filled with hard work and danger offset by a leisurely pace, rolling countryside, and the bonds of love and laughter — is now a secure part of our nation's history.

Glossary

Aqueduct: a large stone structure used to carry water over another body of water or across a valley.

Bogtrotter: a person who lives in or near a bog; commonly used to refer to an Irishman.

Bow: the front of a boat.

Croaker: someone who always predicts that bad things will happen.

Cuddy: a tiny area just behind the boat cabin where the captain and his family or crew slept.

Dowfart: a stupid, dull individual.

Driver: the crew member assigned to control the mules or horses while they are pulling the boat. Drivers were often very young.

Independent Boat: any boat that is owned and captained by an individual.

Lickspigot: a disgusting parasite.

Line or Company Boat: one boat in a fleet owned by a single company.

Locks: a rectangular area large enough to hold a ninety-foot-long boat and used to raise or lower boats over uneven terrain.

Mick: a disparaging term used in reference to an Irishman. It probably came from the nickname for Michael, though when referring to a person it is always spelled with a lower case *m*.

Packet: a canal boat used exclusively to transport people.

Pixilated: anyone who is confused or easily led astray.

Steersman: the individual who controls the rudder or sweep. One who steers the canal barge.

Stern: the back of a boat.

Stoved: when a hole is punched through a boat's hull it is said to be stoved.

Sweep: the rudder of a canal barge. The mechanism for steering.

Teched: (pronounced tetched) crazy, addled, not entirely mentally sound.

Towline: a two-hundred-foot-long rope that allows mules or horses to tow the boat.

Towpath: the narrow dirt strip used by mules and horses and their drivers that runs alongside the canal.

Traces: the harness and other gear worn by mules and horses.

Weigh Station: the place where a boat's cargo is weighed so that its fee for using the canal can be computed.